M. G. LEONARD AND SAM SEDGMAN

Illustrations by
ELISA PAGANELLI

FEIWEL AND FRIENDS
NEW YORK

A FEIWEL AND FRIENDS BOOK
An imprint of Macmillan Publishing Group, LLC
120 Broadway, New York, NY 10271

Our books may be purchased in bulk for promotional, educational, or
business use. Please contact your local bookseller or the Macmillan Corporate
and Premium Sales Department at (800) 221-7945 ext. 5442 or by email at
MacmillanSpecialMarkets@macmillan.com.

Library of Congress Control Number: 2019940848

ISBN 978-1-250-22289-3 (hardcover) / ISBN 978-1-250-22290-9 (ebook)

Book design by Katie Klimowicz

Feiwel and Friends logo designed by Filomena Tuosto

First edition, 2020

1   3   5   7   9   10   8   6   4   2

mackids.com

As for trains—what can beat a train? . . . To travel by train is to see nature and human beings, towns and churches and rivers—in fact, to see life.

Agatha Christie

CHAPTER ONE

TICKET TO RIDE

Harrison Beck pulled a pen from the pocket of his yellow jacket, deftly turning it over his index finger so it was nib down, and began to draw in the central margin of the newspaper spread across the table. The worry lines he saw gouged into his father's forehead were making him nervous.

Colin Beck put down the sports section of the paper with a frustrated sigh and pointed at the station clock. "He said he'd meet us here at five. We're in the café your brother specified; it's five o'clock." He looked out at the people crisscrossing the station. "So where is he, Bev?"

"Don't fret, love," Beverly Beck scolded her husband gently. "It'll give you indigestion." She laid her hand on his sleeve. "Nat'll be here."

Hal's pen twitched as he studied his mother's face. She looked tired. Dad's blue duffle coat drowned her, but she was so pregnant that her bump bulged out the front. No one had asked him if he wanted a baby sister—he was getting one whether he liked it or not. He put down his pen.

1

"Mom, I don't want to go with Uncle Nat. I want to stay with you. I don't like trains. They're boring."

"I know, sausage"—she reached over and ruffled his hair—"but it'll be good for you to spend some time with your uncle. He's an interesting man."

Hal made a face. Whenever a grown-up said something was good for you, that meant it was dull, or disgusting, or both.

"You'd only be stuck in a hospital waiting room, and that's no place for you to end your summer holiday." She patted his hand. "You might even enjoy yourself."

"I won't." Hal looked up through the glass roof of the station at a cloudy sky. He didn't want to be packed off on a train journey with a weird uncle he only ever saw at Christmas. The high brick arches of King's Cross were wrapped in a white latticework sculpture that made the inside of the station feel like a hive, and all the busy passengers, bees. A seething tangle of people rushed about dragging bags and carrying briefcases. A man stood next to a metal rack stacked with newspapers, shoving them at people. Hal glimpsed the headline JEWEL THIEF STRIKES AGAIN as a woman in a suit snatched one from the vendor, flipping it under her armpit to read on the train. Two bulging-breasted pigeons strutted toward him, pecking at the floor.

Colin Beck kicked out his leg. "Get away." He grunted. "Vermin."

Hal frowned at his dad, tearing the crust from his half-eaten ham sandwich and ducking under the table to toss it to the startled-eyed birds. The pigeons grabbed the finger of bread and began a tug-of-war. A pair of sneakers, charcoal suede with three white stripes, stopped beside the table. Hal saw chestnut

2

herringbone trousers with a crisp vertical crease. It could only be one person. Mom's metal chair scraped against the concrete floor as she got up.

"Nat!" she cried, waddling around the table and throwing her arms around her older brother.

"Careful, Bev—you'll knock me over." Uncle Nat put down his battered leather suitcase and umbrella, hugging her. "How are you, pet? Are you well?"

"Yes," Mom replied, her eyes darting to Hal. "I'm fine."

"Nathaniel, good to see you." Dad was on his feet, grabbing Uncle Nat's hand and shaking it. "We appreciate you doing this— we really do."

Hal's eyes flicked from his uncle to his father. Uncle Nat was composed of straight lines. He was thin, had neatly trimmed straight hair, and wore thick-framed tortoiseshell glasses. His crumpet-colored raincoat and mustard sweater went perfectly with his trousers and shoes. By contrast, Dad was a jumble of circles. His kind round face reached up to a receding bowl of salt-and-pepper hair crowned with a bald patch. His shoulders rolled forward, and his navy plaid shirt was tucked into his brown-belted chinos, underlining his overhanging belly.

Uncle Nat turned to Hal, his eyes twinkling. "It's about time I got to know my nephew better." He offered Hal his hand. "You've grown since Christmas, Harrison. Are you excited about our steam-powered adventure?"

Hal shook his uncle's hand and nodded, but he wasn't going to say yes, because that would be a lie. A journey all the way to Scotland and back on the slowest train in the world with his weird uncle was not what he called an adventure.

"Are you sure you're all right with Hal coming with you?" Mom said, picking up Hal's rucksack and slipping it onto his shoulders. "I've told him to give you space when you need to work."

Uncle Nat was a travel writer, and he'd agreed to bring Hal along with him on a work trip, while Beverly Beck went to the hospital to have the baby.

"Absolutely. Don't worry about us." Uncle Nat placed a careful hand on his sister's bump. "You concentrate on bringing this baby out into the world safely. I expect all three of you to be at Paddington station to meet us on our return, in four days."

"Yes." Hal nodded furiously. His mouth moved, but no other words came out.

"I'm going to be all right, Hal," his mom said softly. She bent down, putting her hand to his cheek. "You mustn't worry. Your dad'll look after me." She undid the silver chain that hung around her neck. "Here, take Grandad's Saint Christopher for good luck. The patron saint of travelers will keep you safe on your journey."

Hal gripped the silver medallion between his thumb and forefinger. He felt the engraving of Saint Christopher, staff in hand, child on shoulders. "But what if you need it?"

"You can give it back to me when you get home." She fastened the necklace and then fussed with his jacket, pulling out the hood where it had gathered under his rucksack. She ran the tips of her fingers through his ash-blond hair. "You'll be a good boy for your uncle, won't you?"

"Yes, Mom."

"What route is the Highland Falcon taking, Nathaniel?" his dad asked.

"We'll be traveling up the east coast to Balmoral, where we'll stop for lunch tomorrow, before looping round Scotland and back down the west."

Hal's dad nodded. "They've spent days putting up decorations in Crewe. The station looked impressive when we got the train down today."

"I expect there'll be lots of ceremonial pomp." Uncle Nat winked at Hal. "This will be a journey you'll remember for the rest of your life."

"You're lucky to be going on this trip, son." Hal's dad patted his shoulder. "When I were a lad, I remember waving to the Highland Falcon as she passed through Crewe. She's a lovely-looking locomotive."

"I'm going to miss you." Hal's mom hugged him. "Do as your uncle says, and we'll see you in four days."

"We're going to have fun." Uncle Nat picked up his suitcase, hooked his umbrella over his arm, and took hold of Hal's hand. "Right, we've got to get a move on. We don't want to miss our train."

Hal struggled to speak. He hadn't said goodbye properly.

His parents drew back, waving and smiling as Uncle Nat pulled him across the concourse. He saw his father put a protective arm around his mother. They turned and walked into the crowd, and—just like that—they were gone.

"You're going to need your ticket." Uncle Nat let go of Hal and reached into the pocket of his raincoat.

Scanning the crowd for a glimpse of his parents, Hal saw only the blank faces of strangers. His insides felt hollow. Uncle Nat pressed a white rectangle into his hand.

"Are you ready, Harrison?" His voice was soft, like Hal's mom's.

Hal glanced over his shoulder, then looked up at his uncle and nodded. "I'm ready."

A crowd of people were gathered by the platform entrance, jostling for position.

"Let's not dawdle on the red carpet," Uncle Nat said, striding toward them. "We'll leave the stage for those who like the spotlight."

Looking down at his yellow jacket and faded blue jeans, Hal felt a jolt of panic. He wasn't wearing the right clothes for walking on a red carpet.

"Tickets, please," a uniformed guard said. Hal held out the white card with his name on it. Cameras flashed, and the guard smiled. "Welcome, Harrison Beck, to the final journey of the Highland Falcon."

CHAPTER TWO

THE HIGHLAND FALCON

T he first thing Hal saw was a glittering greenhouse on wheels. The bottom half of the carriage was varnished wood, the top half, sparkling rectangles of glass held in place by gold rods that arched up and over the train. Inside he could see lush green tropical plants.

"What kind of train has a greenhouse?"

"That's an observation car," Uncle Nat said with a grin. "It's for admiring the scenery. As we chuff down the tracks, we'll be able to enjoy the late-summer colors of the country-side or gaze out at the North Sea. You might catch a glimpse of the kraken."

"The kraken isn't real." Hal didn't believe in sea monsters; he was nearly twelve.

"Really? Well then, when it gets dark, you can lie on one of the sofas and look up at the stars."

A cry went up. Hal turned and saw a woman sashaying along the red carpet in a forget-me-not-blue dress. She looked over her shoulder at the cameras, pouting her red lips and throwing her head back, laughing at nothing.

Hal gasped. "Sierra Knight! What's she doing here?"

But Uncle Nat was striding away from the red carpet and didn't reply.

"Sierra Knight's famous." Hal ran to catch up with his uncle. "She's a movie star."

"Sierra Knight is one of the guests," Uncle Nat replied. "She's part of the grand tour."

"Sierra Knight is coming on the train with us? No way!" Hal couldn't wait to tell his best friend, Ben, about this. He'd swallow his own tongue with jealousy—he had a mega crush on Sierra Knight. "What happens on a grand tour, Uncle Nat? What do we do?"

"We live, eat, and sleep in one of the finest trains ever created," Uncle Nat said, "and we stay out of trouble. We're lucky we're nobodies. Nobodies have no formal duties. The royal couple have to do all the hard work."

"Royal couple?"

"Didn't your mom tell you that you were coming with me on the *royal* steam train?"

"I wasn't listening," Hal admitted. "I wanted to stay and help Dad take care of Mom."

8

Uncle Nat put his hand on Hal's shoulder and leaned down. "Do you know what would help your mom more than anything?"

"Me being out of the way." Hal looked at the floor.

"No. You having a great holiday with me and coming back with stories to tell her while she recovers. There will be plenty of opportunities to look after her when we're back. What will make your mom happy is knowing that you're happy. Isn't it?"

Hal nodded begrudgingly.

"So chin up. Time to start enjoying yourself. Look at that veranda." His uncle pointed the tip of his umbrella at a platform extending from the observation car. "Exquisite ironwork. See the floral motif around the royal crest? Fantastic."

Hal looked at the metal and wondered if his uncle wasn't a little bit crazy. "Um, yeah—fantastic ironwork."

"Once the royal couple has boarded at Balmoral, the Highland Falcon will slow down to a walking pace when it travels through a station. The prince and princess will stand on the veranda waving at well-wishers, celebrating their recent wedding." He lifted a finger, and a porter scurried over.

"Yes, sir?" The porter bobbed his head.

"Compartment nine, please." Uncle Nat took Hal's rucksack from his back, putting it down beside his suitcase. "Now, Harrison, before getting under steam, I always pay a visit to the loco—that's short for locomotive." He raised the point of his umbrella. *"To the engine!"* As they marched along the platform, Uncle Nat threw out his hand. "Look! Pullman carriages—the height of luxury."

Hal had never seen an adult so in love with a train before, and he found himself smiling as his uncle enthusiastically spouted facts about it.

Uncle Nat stopped dead, and Hal bumped into his back. "You see that red? That's claret—the shade of the royal family's livery. You won't see another train this color."

Hal stared at it. The dense red felt rich with power and the blood of history.

"This carriage," his uncle continued, "is the King Edward Saloon. It was built before the war, for King George V. It has a wonderful library, as well as card tables and a dartboard."

"Dartboard? Isn't that dangerous on a moving train?"

"Of course. Much more fun. This is the dining car, where we'll eat breakfast, lunch, and dinner, and where we board the train, through those double doors."

A tall man in a burgundy suit with gold buttons and gold-trimmed pockets and lapels stepped forward.

"Mr. Bradshaw, sir." The man dipped his peaked cap. "It's always a pleasure to have you aboard."

"Hello, Gordon. This is my nephew, Harrison Beck. Harrison, this is Gordon Goulde, head steward on the royal train."

"Welcome, Master Beck," Gordon Goulde said, exposing a row of horse teeth.

"Gordon, I want to take Harrison down to the loco. We've time, don't we?"

"If you're quick, sir."

"We'll be back in two winks of a mole's eye." Uncle Nat put a hand on Hal's back and steered him away from the dining car. "Our sleeping compartment will be somewhere in these guest carriages."

"What's that one?" Hal pointed ahead to a carriage with gold-rimmed windows.

"The royal carriages," said Uncle Nat. "Out-of-bounds to us commoners. They'll be empty until we get to Balmoral."

Hal caught his reflection in one of the gold-rimmed windows—springy blond hair, ordinary face, yellow jacket. He wasn't posh enough for this train.

The curtain of the window twitched, startling him. "Aargh!" As he jumped back, he glimpsed fingers, a button nose, and green eyes—but then they were gone.

"You all right?" Uncle Nat looked amused.

"Yeah." Hal blushed. "Uh, how did that head steward man know your name?"

"This isn't my first trip on the Highland Falcon," Uncle Nat said. "I'm a travel writer, but my specialty is trains. I love these marvelous machines." He tapped a finger to his temple. "I've memorized all the historic routes. If I can't sleep, I recite the stations, and before I've reached the end of the line, I've dropped off." He looked delighted.

"Writing about trains—is that a real job?"

Uncle Nat laughed. "I've written about the Highland Falcon before, which is why I've been invited back." He stared along the length of the train to the plumes of dove-gray smoke dancing about the engine's funnel. "I'm grateful to be given the opportunity to say a proper goodbye to this train. She's very special." He gave himself a little shake. "Come on—we must be quick. These last carriages are the service cars for the crew, and there's the tender."

"What's a tender?"

"The truck where the coal and water are stored."

Hal looked at the skip-sized truck and saw a small door in the wall. He blinked as it opened a fraction, and the top part of a face—dark hair and green eyes—peeped out at him and then disappeared. It was the same face he'd seen in the royal carriage.

"Coal?" Hal asked.

"Of course, coal. What do you think a steam train runs on?"

"Steam?"

"And how is the steam made, Harrison? Eh?"

"With coal?"

"Precisely. With coal." Uncle Nat waved him forward. "Come on—let's look her right in the face."

The proud engine was a burnished claret, its roof a brilliant white. The streamlined nose of the loco dipped like a hawk's beak. The skirt of the casing lifted on both sides, snarl-like, revealing three giant black wheels. Steam escaped from hidden pipes, hissing threateningly. Water vapor surrounded the engine in a low cloud. Hal felt the urge to pull out his pen and draw the engine, but he had no paper.

"You would have to look for a long time to find an engine more impressive and downright beautiful than this one." Uncle Nat walked toward the nose of the train and laid his hand on it, patting it as if it were a horse.

Copying his uncle, Hal laid his hand on the metal casing and was surprised to find it was warm and vibrating. The locomotive sighed out a puff of steam, as if it were alive—a dragon, ancient, powerful, and ready to fly.

CHAPTER THREE

DIAMOND DOGS

"Gentlemen." The train guard appeared. "I'll be blowing my whistle in seven minutes."

"Thank you, Graham." Uncle Nat saluted.

A lightning storm of camera flashes blinded Hal as they hurried back along the platform. Standing on the red carpet was a silver-haired woman in a Robin Hood hat garnished with a long pheasant feather. An astonishing number of pearl necklaces hung around her neck, draping over her tweed hunting jacket. She moved her gloved hand in a circular motion, giving the paparazzi a steely smile.

"Keep up," Uncle Nat called, as he stepped up into the dining car, passing his coat and umbrella to the head steward.

Hal walked backward to the train, unable to take his eyes off the five fluffy white dogs with diamond-studded collars behind the silver-haired lady. A red-faced man with mousy-brown bangs was clinging to their leashes, trying to control them.

Hal loved dogs. Every birthday and Christmas, he begged for one, but his parents always refused. They said dogs were expensive and a big responsibility. When they'd told him he was going to have a little sister, he'd asked how they could afford another human but not a dog, especially since children were an even bigger responsibility than a dog. He hadn't meant to be rude, but he found himself being sent to his room anyway.

Stepping into the dining car was like stepping back in time. Neat dining tables draped with white linen tablecloths and flanked with high-backed armchairs were set on opposite sides of the aisle, like a curious narrow restaurant. The air was heavy with furniture polish.

"What are you staring at?" Uncle Nat asked.

Hal pointed out the window. "Imagine being rich enough to have five dogs."

"That's the Countess of Arundel, Lady Elizabeth Lansbury—one of the wealthiest women in England. I met her recently at the Duchess of Kent's gala. A very impressive woman."

"Do you think she'll bring her dogs on the train?"

"I hope she doesn't," said a reedy voice. "I'm allergic to them."

"Ernest White." Uncle Nat crossed the carriage and grasped the hand of an old man wearing a gray wool suit. He was seated at one of the tables reading a newspaper through half-moon spectacles. "What a treat to see you."

"Always a pleasure, young Nathaniel." Ernest White smiled. "Quite the commotion out there, isn't it?" He looked over his spectacles at Hal. "Is this your boy?"

"My nephew, Harrison."

Hal smiled politely.

"I have a grandson called Harrison." Ernest shook his hand. "He works on the Caledonian Sleeper. Son of my youngest daughter—she drives freight trains up in Scotland."

"I didn't realize you'd be joining the royal tour, Ernest. Not working, I hope?" Uncle Nat sank into the armchair opposite Ernest.

"Lord, no. Too old now." Ernest looked over at Hal. "I was the head steward on the royal train for forty-seven years." He sighed. "Some of the happiest moments of my life were on this train." He turned back to Uncle Nat. "They knew I'd want to say goodbye to her. I was so pleased when I got the invitation." The old man's eyes filled up. "It means a lot."

Not wanting to stare, Hal looked down at Ernest White's newspaper.

There was a fuss behind him as Lady Lansbury swept into the dining car.

"*Ghastly* people!" She threw her hands in the air. "One photograph is never enough for those beasts." She disappeared through the door at the other end of the carriage, leaving the man with her dogs struggling to get them onto the train unassisted.

Day by Da

THIEF STRIKES AGAIN

Priceless ruby ring stolen at charity benefit gala. Baroness of Kent offers **£10,000 REWARD** for information that leads to an arrest.

"They're Samoyeds!" Hal said excitedly, holding out his hand to the closest one, who promptly licked it.

The dogs' fluffy white tails wagged as they poked their noses into corners, seeking interesting smells. The dog handler cursed as he was pulled in different directions. Hal tried to help, pulling one out from under a table. It jumped up and licked his face.

"Heel!" shouted the dog handler, and the dogs scrabbled back to him. He herded them through the carriage, following Lady Lansbury.

"I wonder what their names are," Hal said.

"That's Baron Wolfgang Essenbach," Uncle Nat said, "and his youngest son, Milo."

Hal thought his uncle had meant the dogs, until an imposing man with dark, gray-streaked hair wearing a midnight-blue waistcoat stepped onto the train. Behind him came a tall, glowering figure, all elbows and shoulders. Gordon Goulde welcomed the two men onto the train, ushering them in the direction of the observation car.

"The baron is an old friend of His Royal Highness the Prince," Ernest White whispered, "and a great rail enthusiast."

Hal recognized the next guest stepping onto the train. Steven Pickle was a rich entrepreneur who ran lots of companies, including a train company called Grailax, but he was famous for being on a reality TV program. Clinging to his arm was a curvaceous red-haired woman with a fake tan. Hal supposed she must be his wife. Reaching into his pocket, Hal toyed with his pen; he was itching to draw the guests. Steven Pickle's skin looked like uncooked sausage meat. He had salami for arms and chipolata fingers.

"I don't believe it," Ernest White hissed. "Who invited those parasites?"

"Evening." Steven Pickle greeted them with a nod. "It's not bad for an antique, is it?" His beady eyes flickered about the carriage. "Could do with modernizing."

Uncle Nat placed a restraining hand on Ernest's arm.

17

"I'm Lydia Pickle." His wife smiled generously, her red lips lifting like a theater curtain to reveal ultra-white capped teeth. "Nice to meet you."

Mr. Pickle's mobile rang. He pulled it from his pocket and shouted into the phone. "Hello? No. I'm busy. Call me back."

"Lovely to meet you, Lydia," Uncle Nat replied, shaking her hand as she fluttered her false eyelashes at him. "I'm Nathaniel Bradshaw, and this is my nephew, Harrison."

Gordon Goulde shut the double doors of the dining car, dropping a brass bar across them. The piercing sound of a whistle made them all look up.

"Thirty-four minutes past," said Ernest White, checking his watch and tutting. "Four minutes behind schedule already."

Hal felt a jolt and a thrill as the train began to move. The photographers on the platform surged toward them.

"Quick, Harrison." Uncle Nat rose. "Let's go to the observation car and wave King's Cross goodbye."

CHAPTER FOUR

A GRAND DEPARTURE

Hal followed Uncle Nat as he dashed through the King Edward Saloon, past the library and game room, and into the glass carriage. Outside, people were running along the platform, waving. Sierra Knight stood on the veranda, blowing kisses. The whistle tooted twice as King's Cross retreated. The actress pivoted and came inside. A friendly-looking blond woman brought Sierra a drink. Hal instinctively liked her because, other than a sparkling bracelet, she was dressed in an ordinary blouse and skirt, the kind his mother might wear. She looked normal. Everyone else was dressed as if they were at a fancy party.

A waitress stood beside a trolley covered with a white cloth, handing out drinks.

"Nathaniel!" A tall man with a shaven head and a camera slung around his neck crossed the carriage with an outstretched hand. "My old friend." The man clasped Uncle Nat's hand.

"Isaac!" Uncle Nat smiled at the lean man. "You're a sight for sore eyes. Harrison, meet Isaac Adebayo. He's a royal photographer. We've known each other for years, ever since we

19

covered the Queen's Golden Jubilee tour on the Duchess of Sutherland."

"Now *that's* a magnificent train," Isaac said.

"Not a patch on the Highland Falcon, though," Uncle Nat said, and the two men began to chat in earnest about their favorite locomotives.

Hal looked around. All the guests appeared to be gathering in the glass carriage. His heart sank as he realized they were all adults.

The baron and his son stood together. Hal noticed Milo Essenbach had a scar from his nostril down to his top lip, which gave him a perpetual snarl. The man sensed his gaze and looked over at Hal, who looked at the floor. "Uncle Nat, I'm going to get an orange juice," he said, and Uncle Nat nodded.

As he crossed the carriage, Hal thought about the face he'd glimpsed through the window of the royal carriage. It hadn't looked like an adult. Hal wished he still had his rucksack so he could shrink into a corner and play his game console, but it had been taken to the compartment by the porter. The waitress smiled at him as he took a glass of juice.

TING! TING! Baron Essenbach stepped forward with a raised champagne glass and spoke to the room in an elegant German accent.

"In the absence of His Royal Highness the Prince, I propose we must lift high our glasses to this outstanding example of human engineering and design that is the Highland Falcon. We celebrate the place of the locomotive in the industrial revolution, and its impact on the economic infrastructure of your great country." He paused to take a breath.

"Oh, yes, we must!" Sierra twirled so that she came to a halt between the baron and his son with her glass held high. "Here's to a simply darling train and gorgeous company on our adventure around the British Isles." She fluttered her eyelashes at the baron and then his son before turning back to the carriage full of people. She opened her mouth to continue, just as Lady Lansbury stalked in and marched toward Hal, her black dangly earrings swinging as she reached past him for a glass of champagne and lifted it.

Hal felt suddenly exposed standing next to Lady Lansbury, and he shuffled backward into the corner and sank down into a chair, wondering why adults liked speeches so much.

"In memory of those who dedicated their lives to the railway, like my dearly departed George, the Count of Arundel. May the final journey of this historic train emblazon the steam locomotive on the lion hearts of the people of the United Kingdom, for humanity did something remarkable when it produced the steam locomotive. It changed the world forever." She raised her glass. "The Highland Falcon."

"The Highland Falcon," everyone repeated.

"Bottoms up!" Lydia Pickle cried, emptying her glass in one gulp.

Hal blinked. From his seat, he could see the white cloth on the drinks trolley rising. He saw dark hair, brown skin, green eyes, and then the whole face of a girl about his age. He froze, not wanting to move in case she disappeared. He watched her scan the room, and then she looked his way. Their eyes met. She stuck out her tongue and dropped the tablecloth.

Springing up, Hal lurched forward as Steven Pickle stepped in front of him.

"Oof, sorry," Hal said, as they collided.

Mr. Pickle looked like he was going to shout at Hal, but his phone rang, and he turned away to answer it. "Hello? No! I told you. I'm busy!"

"S'all right, love." Lydia Pickle wrinkled her nose as she winked, smiling at Hal. "I keep doing that, too." She pointed at her leopard-print shoes with very high heels. "Nightmare!" She grabbed on to Steven Pickle's arm, clutching her empty glass to her bosom. As she tottered forward, the glass clinked against a gaudy bow of sparkling diamonds pinned to her chest.

Hal looked past her to the trolley as Lady Lansbury approached Baron Essenbach, who was now talking to Uncle Nat in the middle of the carriage. The Pickles joined them. Hal seized his opportunity and darted around the group.

"Would you like some more orange juice?" the waitress asked.

Hal nodded. "Yes, please." He looked down. "Oh, my shoe-lace is undone." He bent down, pretending to tie his sneakers, and lifted the corner of the white cloth, expecting to see the girl—but no one was there. He stood up and looked around. Where could she have gone?

"There you are," Uncle Nat said, suddenly beside him. "Shall we go and dress for dinner?"

"Dress for dinner?" Hal thought about the clothes he'd put in his rucksack and knew instinctively that his jeans, sweatpants, and sweaters weren't going to be appropriate.

"Yes, and we haven't explored our room yet." Uncle Nat looked like an excited child.

"Right." Hal nodded, following his uncle to the door.

"Oh! It's gone!" squawked Lydia Pickle. She fell to all fours, crawling around on the floor. "My brooch! I've lost it!"

Steven Pickle grunted, sitting down beside Ernest White, who turned away and glared out the window. There was a flash of light in the glass as Isaac snapped a photograph of Sierra. On the other side of the carriage, Lady Lansbury was having a conversation with Baron Essenbach in fluent German, while Milo Essenbach stood by looking murderous.

Uncle Nat rolled his eyes and mouthed, *Let's go!*

As Hal left the observation car, he looked back at the trolley. *Whoever that girl is*, he thought, *I'm going to find her.*

In the King Edward Saloon, away from the chatter of the party, Hal could hear the rhythmic clatter of wheels on rails. He ran his fingers along the felt cloth of the billiard table and eyed the dartboard. *I wonder if that girl plays darts.* He'd like to try to throw darts on a rocking train.

Uncle Nat scanned the titles of the leather-bound books as they passed through the library, and beyond it they found a lounge furnished with two card tables, each with two decks. Hal thought the train journey might not be so boring if he had someone his own age to play with, and he wondered why the girl was hiding.

Back in the dining car, Hal spotted Ernest White's newspaper. He picked it up as they walked past, curious about the jewel thief. There was a cubbyhole of a kitchen at the end of the carriage, and beyond it were the guest compartments.

"Number nine. This is us," Uncle Nat said.

Hal pushed the slim wooden door and stepped into a beautifully decorated compartment. Along the right wall of the room stretched a settee of ocean-blue tapestry shot through with gold, on which

23

his rucksack and Uncle Nat's suitcase and coat sat. "Where are the beds?"

"Train compartments are a box of delights." Uncle Nat pointed to a tiny porcelain sink tucked away in the left corner, behind the door. A thin gold mixer tap arched over the bowl. "Running hot and cold water, a gentleman's shaving mirror on an expandable bracket"—he stretched it out like a concertina—"and a glass shelf for toiletries." He grabbed a wooden handle, lifting a rolling sheet of thin wooden strips up and over the top of a wardrobe rail, exposing seven gold hangers. "For shirts and jackets." He pointed down. "And three drawers for underwear and socks."

Uncle Nat took a step to his right. "Here, an essential item of furniture." He lifted a catch, and a wooden desktop dropped down out of the wall, its surface covered with the same blue leather as the chair positioned below it. Uncle Nat transferred his suitcase to the desk and tucked the wooden chair under. "I sleep there," he said, pointing at the couch. "And you"—he slipped off his sneakers and stepped onto the seat cushion—"will sleep here." He unhooked a latch, and a bunk dropped down, held at ninety degrees by two leather straps that were bolted to the wall.

"Epic." Hal grinned.

"Or rather, compact, but I get your meaning!" Uncle Nat's glasses lifted as he smiled. "Under the bottom bunk is a drawer— you can put your things in there." He held out his hands. "What more could two travelers need?"

"Actually"—Hal shuffled from one foot to the other—"there might be something I need. I don't think I brought the right clothes for dinner."

"I'm sure we can fix that." Uncle Nat pushed a gold button above the writing desk.

London

Hal wondered if a secret door was going to open and throw a shirt at him, but nothing happened. Uncle Nat took off his mustard sweater.

"You're wearing six watches!"

Uncle Nat looked down at the three wristwatches on each arm. "An idiosyncrasy of mine when I'm working." He pointed first at his left wrist. "This one has the time in London, this one New York, and this one is Tokyo." He pointed to his right. "This has Berlin, Sydney, and Moscow."

"Why?"

"I bought each one on a different journey," Uncle Nat said. "It helps me to be aware of the whole world—not just me in my own time and place. It's good to remember that there are other places on the planet, filled with wonderful people. I like to consider what they might be doing—are they rising with the rosy-fingered dawn, while I am gazing at the stars?"

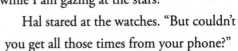

New York

Moscow

Hal stared at the watches. "But couldn't you get all those times from your phone?"

Uncle Nat pulled a gray rectangle from his trouser pocket. "I have an analog phone. It's hard to have an adventure with a smartphone in your pocket. The hypnotic device

26

Berlin

stops you from reading real maps and talking to people. I don't want to stare at a screen. I want to look at the landscape. I want to see the world."

There was a knock.

"You rang, sir?" Gordon Goulde was standing in the doorway.

"Harrison needs a shirt for dinner," Uncle Nat said. "He neglected to pack one. He may need trousers and a tie, too, if you have them."

Hal smiled apologetically.

"I'll see what I can do, sir."

While they waited, Uncle Nat put on tan brogues and a jacket to match his trousers.

Unzipping his rucksack, Hal pulled out his game console and charger. He opened the drawer under the settee and turned his bag upside down, tipping jeans, boxer shorts, socks, T-shirts, and a maroon-and-navy-striped sweater into it. Closing the drawer with his foot, he looked around. "Where are the plugs?"

Tokyo

"What do you need a plug for?" Uncle Nat asked, tying a silk scarf around his neck and tucking it into his open shirt collar.

"To charge my game console." Hal held it up. "I used up the battery on the journey from Crewe."

Sydney

"I'm sorry—I don't think you'll

be able to charge it in the compartment. It predates electronic devices."

"What about that wire?" Hal pointed up to a cable running along the wall just beneath the ceiling.

"That's the emergency-brake cord. If a passenger needs the train to stop suddenly, they pull that, and we'll grind to a halt. It runs through every carriage on the train."

"Oh." Hal sighed and looked down at his game console.

"You could give it to Gordon and ask him to charge it for you. He could get it back to you tomorrow."

"What if I need it?"

"What do you do at home when you can't play games?"

"Play football"—Hal thought for a minute—"or draw."

"I'm sure we could find you some art materials."

Hal sat down on the sofa feeling deflated.

"There's always billiards or darts," Uncle Nat said cheerfully. "And I can teach you a card game or two, if you'd like?"

Gordon Goulde was back, carrying a pair of oatmeal corduroy trousers, a navy blazer with a tartan lining, and a white shirt, all of which he laid out on the bottom bunk. He produced a maroon bow tie from his pocket, placing it on the neck of the shirt.

"They're not for *me*?" Hal was aghast. "They're gross."

Gordon Goulde raised an eyebrow. "I borrowed these from the royal wardrobe," he replied. "They were once worn by the young princes."

"They are perfect." Uncle Nat put a hand on Gordon's shoulder. "Thank you."

"Um, yes," Hal mumbled. "Thanks."

"I'll need them back when we get to Paddington," Gordon Goulde said as he left.

"Wait . . . Mr. Goulde." Hal stood up. "The other children traveling on the train—could you introduce me to them?"

"I'm afraid there are none."

"I mean, not as guests, but in the crew?"

"Children are not allowed to crew the royal train, Master Beck," he said. "You are the only child aboard the Highland Falcon."

CHAPTER FIVE

A DOG'S DINNER

Gordon Goulde is a liar! Hal thought, as his uncle helped him into the itchy tartan-lined blazer.

"I don't have to wear the bow tie, do I?"

Uncle Nat laughed. "If you don't seize the opportunity to wear a bow tie when you're on a royal train, when will you ever wear one?" He picked it up. "Haven't you ever wondered what it's like to be a prince?"

Hal stared at the maroon bow.

Popping up his collar, Uncle Nat slung the tie around Hal's neck, creating the bow expertly with nimble fingers. Hal looked at himself in the mirror above the sink. He looked posh. If he wore these clothes to school, he'd be bullied for sure.

"Think of it as a costume. Pretend you're

a spy." Uncle Nat waggled his eyebrows. "The name's Beck—Harrison Beck."

I am a spy, Hal thought, staring at his reflection, *and I'm going to find out who that girl is and why Gordon Goulde is lying.* He turned to his uncle. "You know, you don't need to keep calling me Harrison. You can call me Hal. That's what my friends call me."

"Thank you, *Hal*." Uncle Nat beamed. "That means a lot. Now, shall we eat? I'm starving."

The dining car was bustling. The mouthwatering smell of food emanating from the kitchen made Hal's stomach growl. Uncle Nat made a beeline for the table where Isaac the photographer was sitting on his own. Sierra and her blond friend were dining at a table with Steven and Lydia Pickle. Ernest White was across the aisle on his own, and at the farthest table sat the baron and his surly son. As the train swayed, the cutlery and glasses clinked and shuddered, but no one seemed to mind.

"Why is Sierra Knight on the grand tour?" Hal asked, as bowls of steaming soup were placed on the table in front of them.

"She's a friend of the princess," Isaac replied, picking up his spoon. "They worked together, several years back. She says she wanted to come because she's researching a role for a new film about a female train driver in the Second World War."

"Shockingly, there weren't any female train drivers until the 1980s." Uncle Nat shook his head.

"Is her friend an actress, too?" Hal asked.

"That's not her friend," Uncle Nat replied. "That's Lucy Meadows, Sierra Knight's personal assistant."

Hal glanced over. Sierra was gazing out the window. He

wondered what she could be staring at, until she pursed her lips, and he realized it was her own reflection.

"Oh, Lucy." Sierra grabbed her assistant's arm. "Imagine me leaning out of the engine and looking into the camera." She paused, eyes growing wide. "There's such a *freedom* to traveling by train," she proclaimed. Then she smiled, apparently pleased with herself. "That's a good line, don't you think? Write it down. We'll send it to the screenwriter."

Lucy Meadows dutifully took a notebook and pen from her cardigan pocket, while opposite, Steven Pickle slurped his pea soup.

"I love that brooch." Lydia Pickle huffed. "I've never seen a brooch that shape before—a big bow all covered in diamonds. I love bows. The jeweler said it was a one-off. All the girls at the salon love it. It's just so twinkly." She clapped a manicured hand to her forehead. "You'll keep a look out for it, won't you? It cost a mint."

"Of course." Lucy nodded. "We both will. I'm sure it'll turn up."

"I had it on when we were in the greenhouse, glugging the champers, but then I looked down, and it was *gone*!" Lydia stuck out her bottom lip and blinked to show how sad she was.

"You probably weren't even wearing it," grunted Steven Pickle.

"But I *was* wearing it!" Lydia protested. "Didn't you see?"

Hal remembered Lydia's sparkling bow. It had been hard to miss.

"I hope you put it on the insurance," said Steven Pickle, tearing a bread roll.

"'Course I did." Lydia bit her lip and looked away.

As the Highland Falcon rattled through Stevenage, the woman who'd been serving drinks in the observation car wheeled in a trolley carrying a side of beef and carving tools. Hal stared at the trolley's white cloth, looking for signs of movement. When she came to serve their table, he stuck out his foot, pushing the cloth in. There was nothing behind it.

"Hello." He smiled sweetly at the waitress as she served Uncle Nat and Isaac. "What's your name?"

"Amy."

"Do you think I could have an extra Yorkshire pudding, please, Amy?"

"Of course, sir."

The smart blazer and bow tie seemed to be working. "Amy, can I ask you something?"

"Yes, sir."

"Have you seen a girl on the train, about my age?"

Amy looked shocked. "No! You are the only child passenger. There are no children allowed in the crew carriages." She deftly dropped a second Yorkshire pudding onto his plate and hurriedly pushed the trolley to the next table to serve the baron and his son.

Hal narrowed his eyes. She was lying. *No children allowed?* There were secrets everywhere. He looked down at his Yorkshire puddings.

"They won't be as good as your mom's," Uncle Nat said. "No one makes a better pud than Bev."

"Mom's are the best," Hal agreed, "but I'll eat them anyway. I love Yorkshire pudding." He watched Amy serve the baron, who picked up his napkin, flicked it open, and tucked it into the collar of his shirt.

"Did you know, the baron owns the most impressive model railway in the whole of Europe?" Uncle Nat said in a low voice. "He built most of it himself."

33

Isaac nodded. "It is a joy to behold. If you're ever near Hohen-schwangau Castle in Bavaria, you should check it out. He lets the public in on weekends."

"He's a distant relative of the royal family," Uncle Nat said. "I've enjoyed his company a number of times, although I've not met his son before."

Across the aisle, Hal saw Ernest White stand up. He had a foam-headed microphone in his hand and was sliding open the top panel of the window. He clamped the microphone to the window frame, foam end poking out, then plugged it into a small portable tape recorder, which he tucked between the seat and the carriage wall.

"What's Mr. White doing?"

Uncle Nat smiled. "He's recording the sound of the steam train traveling at speed."

Hal frowned. "Why?"

"Because it's unique, and for him it's attached to important memories. The sound of an A4 Pacific under steam is as beautiful to Ernest White as a symphony by Beethoven." Uncle Nat sat back and closed his eyes, listening to the train.

Hal tried to do the same, but all he could hear was Lydia Pickle.

"Last week, I was reading about your breakup with Chad in *Hot Stories* magazine," Lydia Pickle said loudly to Sierra, "and now look at me having a proper meal with you." She shook her head in disbelief. "Is it true you're from Liverpool? You don't have a Scouse accent."

Sierra Knight replied with a tight smile and a tiny nod.

Lydia Pickle held up her hands, squeaking in a high voice, "Eh! Eh! Ferry cross the Mersey."

Steven Pickle roared with laughter at her terrible impression of a Liverpudlian.

Ernest White scowled and shook his head at the noise.

"No one likes Mr. Pickle, do they?" said Hal quietly.

"He makes a great deal of money from the railways but spends very little of it improving them," said Uncle Nat. "That upsets people."

"Who needs trains with *seats*?" Isaac said with a wink. "Or air-conditioning? Or ones that run on time?"

"Why was he invited on this journey, then?"

"Well"—Uncle Nat leaned forward—"he owns quite a bit of the line we're traveling on. Not to invite him would have been an insult, but I think everyone was hoping he wouldn't come."

"But he wants his picture in the papers," Isaac said, giving Hal a knowing look, "standing next to royalty."

Dessert arrived, and Hal wolfed down the sugary pile of strawberry shortcake.

"Where's Lady Lansbury?" he said, looking around. "Isn't she having dinner?"

"In the private dining compartment," Uncle Nat replied. "She's having a personal ceremony to commemorate the passing of her husband, and I believe"—he leaned in and whispered—"scattering his ashes into the steam and the smuts."

"Oh!" Hal was startled.

"She's being served by her gentleman-in-waiting."

"Is that the man who looks after her dogs?"

Uncle Nat chuckled. "I'll bet when he took the job, he didn't realize he'd have to wait on five dogs as well as a countess."

"She must love dogs," Hal said.

"They're a new addition to the household," Isaac said. "She got them after her husband passed away."

If Lady Lansbury and her gentleman-in-waiting were here in the dining car, Hal suddenly realized, the dogs must be on their own in a compartment. "Please may I leave the table? I, um, want to go back and unpack my stuff."

Uncle Nat wiped his mouth with his napkin and nodded. "Would you mind if I stayed for an after-dinner coffee?"

"No." Hal got up. "I'll be fine."

He hurried through the sleeper carriages, listening out for snuffles or woofs. From behind the second-to-last door—number two—he heard scratching, a high-pitched whine, and an excited bark. He looked about, then turned the handle. To his surprise, the door opened.

Five snowy dogs rushed him, and he laughed as they jumped up, pinning him to the door, trying to lick his face. One let out a joyful bark.

"Shhhh!" Hal whispered, slipping into the compartment and sinking to his knees. "You have to be quiet."

The dogs clamored around him in a huddle, nuzzling their heads against his shoulders. He tried to stroke each of them, but they overwhelmed him, and he found himself lying on the floor, giggling as wet noses poked his rib cage looking for a pet and his face got licked.

"Stop it!" He laughed, trying to sit up. "Sit!"

To his surprise, all five dogs obediently sat on their haunches and panted at him with shining eyes.

Hal reached out. "Let's see." He read the silver tags dangling below their diamond-studded collars. The nearest dog was darker than the rest, with oatmeal fur. "You are Trafalgar . . . and you're Viking." Viking barked, as if to agree. "You're Shannon," he said to the dog with a flash of silver to her fur. "You're very pretty, aren't you . . . Fitzroy?" He struggled to grab the tag of the fourth dog, who'd decided to try to dig up the carpet. "And what's your name?"

The last dog was the smallest of the five. All the other dogs had black or brown eyes, but she looked at him with eyes as blue as the sea. He patted his knees, and she placed her head on his lap. He pulled up her tag. "Bailey." He stroked the top of her head. "Well, it's lovely to meet you all."

Viking yipped.

Hal pointed at each dog as he repeated their names. "Trafalgar, Viking, Shannon, Fitzroy, and Bailey."

All five Samoyeds smiled at him, and Hal grinned back. "I'm Hal." He patted his chest, and Bailey licked his face. "You've made a right mess in here, haven't you?"

The carpet and the seat were covered in dog hairs. The top bunk was down and made up as a bed for Lady Lansbury's gentleman-in-waiting. There were five water bowls on the floor below the window. And in the sink, a bag of dog biscuits sat below the glass shelf, which had five octagonal glass bottles with *Gyastara* written on their labels in swirly writing.

Fitzroy padded to the compartment door and scratched at it.

"No, Fitzroy—you mustn't do that," Hal scolded.

Bailey clambered onto his lap and curled up.

"Hello, girl." He stroked her head, and she lifted her nose to nuzzle his palm. As he sank his face into her fluffy neck, his heart lurched at the sound of footsteps approaching. Pushing Bailey off, he scrambled to his feet, looking around in a panic.

There was nowhere to hide.

CHAPTER SIX

THE PHANTOM FEAST

Turning to face the door, Hal quickly prepared his apology and took a deep breath. But the footsteps passed. He lifted the blinds, peeping out into the corridor. Amy, the waitress, was carrying a tray of food into the royal carriage. *But there's no one in there*, Hal thought. *The carriage is empty until Balmoral. Who's Amy taking food to?* He slipped out and tiptoed after her.

The royal carriage had a thick cream carpet, which deadened his footsteps. He was in a lounge with mint-green upholstery and glossy wooden furnishings. He ducked behind the closest chaise longue as Amy disappeared through a door at the other end of the carriage. Cautiously, he crept across the room, opening the door an inch and peering into a long corridor beside private rooms. Halfway down, Amy was placing the tray on the floor. She knocked three times on a door, then turned back toward him.

Hal ran. If he was caught in the royal carriage, he'd be in serious trouble. *Someone's in that room!* he thought.

"Calm down, you horrible things."

Hal slowed at the sound of a man's voice inside compartment

two. The dogs were barking. Creeping past the Samoyeds' compartment, he heard a tearing sound. The door was ajar. He saw dog food pellets rain onto the carpet. The dogs hoovered them up. They were hungry. Lady Lansbury's gentleman-in-waiting was standing with his back to the doorway, holding the bag of food.

"Right, which one of you greedy animals wants this bit of juicy roast beef, eh?"

Viking jumped up at him.

"Good boy, Viking. Go on—eat it all up."

Trafalgar jumped up, too, and the man kicked him away. "Get away. It's not for you."

Trafalgar whined in pain and retreated into the corner of the room, licking his leg.

"You can have the next one."

A fire of indignation flamed in Hal's chest. He wanted to shout at the man, but Amy would arrive any second, and he didn't want to get caught at this end of the carriage.

"What do you think you're doing, kid?"

Hal turned and found himself face-to-face with Steven Pickle, who was standing outside compartment three.

"I . . . I wanted to see the dogs."

"Do you think Lady Lansbury would like a kid sneaking around outside her rooms?"

"No, sir. I mean—I wasn't sneaking . . ." Hal tried to shuffle past Steven Pickle. "I was . . ."

"What's going on?" Lady Lansbury's gentleman-in-waiting came to the door as Amy entered the corridor. Hal was surrounded.

"Ah, Rowan," Steven Pickle grunted. "The kid came to look at the dogs. Or, at least, that's what he says."

Hal nodded, glancing at Amy, who was hovering as far back as she could.

Rowan scowled at Hal down his thin nose. "They're not toys, kid." He ran his fingers through his slicked-back hair. "Go away." He returned to his compartment and shut the door.

"Get back to your own room before you get into hot water." Steven Pickle dismissed Hal with a wave of his chipolata fingers.

Hal scurried away, mentally adding his name to the list of people who didn't like Steven Pickle.

***

Back at their compartment, Hal found Uncle Nat sitting at the writing desk, pen in hand and journal open. He'd pinned a map of the British Isles to the backboard of the desk, marking the Highland Falcon's route in red. Hal saw that in his absence, his bunk had been made up with a duvet and a plump pillow.

"There you are," said his uncle, looking up. "Been exploring?"

"I went to visit the dogs." Hal thought it best to tell his uncle before someone else did. "But Mr. Pickle said I was sneaking about and sent me back." He approached the desk. "Why are you writing in different-colored inks?" He pointed at his uncle's journal. "Is that code?" He stared down at the squiggles on the page.

"That's Teeline. It's a shorthand they teach you at journalism school. It's faster to write, and usually only another journalist can decipher it." Uncle Nat put the lid on his fountain pen. "Laptops are impractical if there's no electricity." He gestured around the room. "Each time I write, I use a different-colored ink so that

41

when I read it, I can see when I've taken a break or where something has changed. All I need to do my job is a notebook and two pens. Which reminds me"—he reached into his case, pulling out a red leather-bound book the size of a passport—"this is for you."

Hal took it from his uncle's outstretched hand. The book was secured with a cord, which Hal released. He flicked through the pages—they were blank, ready for him to draw on. "Thank you."

"Hop into your pajamas, brush your teeth, and take it up to your bunk. I've already broken my promise to your mother about getting you to bed by eight."

As soon as Hal was in his bunk, he opened the sketchbook. He held the pen above the paper for a second, and then drew a pair of dancing eyes.

CHAPTER SEVEN

THE FIRTH OF FORTH

The Highland Falcon pulled her sleeping passengers through the dark, tossing steam over their heads like fleeting dreams as she climbed the East Coast Main Line. The shutters of level crossings bowed as she approached the ghostly cobweb of roads around towns. A little after midnight, her brakes sang gently, and she halted in a siding to take on coal and water. With a tender full of fuel, and her pipes hissing fresh steam, the Highland Falcon clanked back onto the main line, steaming toward Scotland.

"Hal, wake up. You've got to see this."

It was light. Hal blinked, opening his eyes. Uncle Nat beckoned him down from his bunk. The blinds were up, and the curtains open. Hal saw a clear expanse of blue, stretching to the horizon. He pressed his face into the glass and realized that they were traveling across a giant bridge made from a lattice of red iron that stretched as far as he could see in either direction.

"Where are we?"

"North of Edinburgh"—Uncle Nat pulled the window

down—"crossing over the Firth of Forth." He put his head out and shouted, "Take a look at this!"

Wriggling in between his uncle and the windowsill, Hal stuck his head out.

"The Forth Bridge!" Uncle Nat whooped. "One of the greatest railway bridges in the world!"

The Highland Falcon blew her whistle, and Hal felt a thrill as the train rocketed across the high bridge, the water shimmering far below. In the distance, the river became the sea, rolling out to meet a bright blue sky. The rhythmic clatter of the train on the rails made the ironwork of the bridge vibrate and ring.

"More than one and a half miles long," Uncle Nat shouted, "and four thousand men to build it. Blooming marvelous."

They ducked their heads back inside, and Uncle Nat shut the window. "You're covered in coal smuts!" He chuckled, turning Hal to face the mirror.

Hal laughed. "So are you!"

Uncle Nat handed him a hot washcloth, and he wiped his face.

"We'll be arriving at Ballater, the station nearest Balmoral

Castle, around midday. We probably won't eat lunch till nearly two," said Uncle Nat. "We'll need a hearty breakfast."

***

In the dining car, Steven Pickle stood nose-to-nose with Gordon Goulde.

"If she had *lost* it"—he jabbed a finger at Gordon's shoulder to punctuate the word—"it would have been found by now. It's not in our compartment, so it must've been nicked!"

"Is there a problem?" Uncle Nat asked.

"You bet there's a problem," Steven Pickle growled. "I was telling Jobsworth here that I want the train searched. One of his crooked crew has pocketed my wife's diamond brooch!"

"All my attendants have a long history of serving the royal f-family," stammered Gordon. "They're completely trustworthy."

"Someone's pinched it," snarled Steven Pickle, stepping back. He looked at Hal, narrowing his eyes. "And when I catch them, I'm going to wring their neck."

He stomped away, plonking himself down at a table, opposite his wife, who was wearing sunglasses.

Wheat fields framed by beech hedgerows rolled past the windows as Hal and his uncle ordered breakfast. Hal was sketching the Forth Bridge when Lady Lansbury arrived in a cloud of white dogs, greeting everyone cheerfully as she sailed through the carriage. Hal reached out under the table and ruffled

Bailey's fur as she passed. He turned over to a clean page and started to draw the dog.

"It's disgusting," Steven Pickle grumbled loudly to Lady Lansbury, his knife and fork clattering down onto his plate. "We're victims of a crime, and no one is doing anything about it. My wife's a wreck."

Lydia nodded but didn't lift her sunglasses.

"My dear," said Lady Lansbury, placing a hand on her shoulder. "Are you unwell?"

"Sick to my stomach," Lydia replied. "Remember my twinkling bow? The one with the emerald that I was wearing last night? It's gone. Stolen."

"Cost me the price of a house, that thing," Steven Pickle grumbled.

"Oh my!" Lady Lansbury's hand went to her throat. "Are you quite sure?"

"Positive!" Steven Pickle replied for his wife. "Aren't you?"

Lydia opened her mouth, but he kept on talking.

"I'm not happy, Lady Lansbury—not happy at all—because *someone* forgot to add it to our insurance. Still, no one pilfers from a Pickle and gets away with it."

Lady Lansbury pursed her lips and looked around. "Well, I wasn't going to say anything, but your troubles make me bold enough to share something odd that has happened to me." She paused. "I, *too*, appear to have lost some valuable jewelry. It was in my vanity case, but now, well, it seems to have gone missing."

Lydia Pickle gasped. "No way! Then there *is* a thief on the train."

"Rowan Buck, my gentleman-in-waiting, looked everywhere this morning—I can be quite a scatterbrain—and, of course, I have so many jewels, it's common for me to lose one or two from time to time. But after hearing your story . . . well—now I'm wondering."

"What did they take?"

"My pearl earrings. A beautiful pair of natural pearls the size of blueberries in antique diamond settings. I was wearing them last night at dinner."

"Oh!" Lydia squealed. "That's when my brooch went missing. Last night, before dinner!"

Steven Pickle swiveled in his seat and pointed at Hal. "You were loitering outside Lady Lansbury's compartment last night. I saw you."

All the passengers in the dining car fell silent and looked at Hal, and he felt himself go bright red.

"I *caught* him sneaking about," Steven Pickle continued.

"I . . ." Hal's voice stuck in his throat.

"Did you take something from my room, young man?" Lady Lansbury asked. "As a game, perhaps? If you did, it would be best to own up now."

Hal shook his head. "I wanted to see your dogs." His head felt hot. "I love dogs."

"He's lying," Steven Pickle said.

Lady Lansbury narrowed her eyes.

"Now then, let's not get ahead of ourselves." Uncle Nat stood up. His voice was calm and reasonable. "I suggest that you both report your suspected crimes to the police once we arrive at Ballater and allow the proper authorities to look into the matter." He nodded and sat down to show that the conversation was finished.

"I'm watching you," Steven Pickle growled at Hal. "Thieving little brat."

"Mr. Pickle, if you level one more accusation at my nephew, I will report you to the police for harassment." Uncle Nat calmly folded his napkin. "Now let that be an end to the matter."

Steven Pickle opened his mouth to say something and then shut it. He picked up his fork and stabbed it into a piece of black pudding on his plate.

"Gordon." Uncle Nat called over the head steward. "We'll take breakfast in our room this morning, please."

"Of course, sir."

***

"I didn't steal anything, Uncle Nat—I promise," Hal said as soon as they were safely back in their compartment.

"Of course you didn't," said Uncle Nat. "I know that. Mr. Pickle is a buffoon and a bully. Lydia Pickle probably misplaced the brooch. It will turn up in their compartment. You'll see."

Breakfast arrived on a tray with fold-down legs, just like the one Hal had seen Amy leave outside the door in the royal carriage yesterday.

"What if there *is* a jewel thief?" Hal said, picking up the newspaper. "Look at this. It says someone's stealing precious jewels from high-society people in London. What if the thief is on board the train?"

"Well, if they are, we've nothing to worry about," said Uncle Nat, as he poured them out a glass of orange juice each. "We haven't got anything worth stealing."

"But, if there is a thief . . . shouldn't we try to catch them?"

"Hal, in a few short hours, the prince and princess will be boarding this train with their royal guard. Only a lunatic would steal from such a secure place." Uncle Nat took a bite of his toast. "Trust me—there are no thieves on this train."

CHAPTER EIGHT

A ROYAL STOWAWAY

After finishing his breakfast, Hal got to his feet, brushing the crumbs from his lap. "I'm going to see if anyone will play darts with me." He grabbed his sketchbook and slid his pen down the spine.

"Would you mind if I didn't join you?" Uncle Nat lifted his journal out from his case. "I have work to do, documenting last night's departure."

"No—that's fine with me." Hal smiled, holding up the sketchbook. "If no one wants a game of darts, I'll do some drawing."

"We'll be passing Dundee soon, crossing over the Tay. There's a grand view from the bridge—keep an eye out."

"I will." Hal slipped the book into the back pocket of his jeans and opened the door.

"If you have any trouble from Mr. Pickle, you come and get me."

"I'll keep out of his way."

"You'd better stay away from Lady Lansbury's dogs, too."

Hal closed the door, took five paces forward, paused, and then tiptoed backward, turning and running toward the royal carriages.

49

"There *is* a jewel thief on this train," he whispered to himself, "and I know exactly where she's hiding."

As he ran, Hal thought about Amy delivering that tray of food. Was she the thief's accomplice? If so, the girl and possibly the stolen jewels were in that royal carriage. If he caught the thief and found the jewels, he might get the reward mentioned in the paper. *Then I could definitely get a dog.*

Putting his fingers into the brass niche of the connecting door to the royal carriage, he slid it sideways. The runners were well oiled and made no sound. Slipping through, his heart po-goed about in his chest as he tiptoed across the spongy carpet to the spot where Amy had left the tray. He pressed his ear to the door, but the beating of his heart was so loud, he couldn't hear anything. He turned the handle silently, opening it a crack. The room was dark. He smelled talcum powder and perfume. He saw a double bed. It was empty, but its covers were rumpled. On the bedside table was a half-full glass of orange juice.

Hal stepped into the room, treading on playing cards laid out in columns. Someone had been playing solitaire. The compartment was empty. He pulled out his sketchbook, sat on the edge of the bed, and drew a quick diagram of the layout of the room.

There was a click as the door swung shut behind him.

"Gotcha!" a voice shouted.

Hal nearly jumped out of his skin. Standing in front of the door, dressed in a black T-shirt and blue overalls, her arms folded across her chest, was the girl who had stuck her tongue out at him. Strapped around her hips was a tool belt. He could see a wrench, two screwdrivers, and a Swiss Army knife. *That's how she got into Lady Lansbury's compartment,* Hal thought. *She picked the lock.*

"No—*I've* caught *you*," Hal said, hastily shoving his sketchbook into his back pocket.

The girl, who was taller than Hal, fixed him with a defiant stare. "Who are you? And what are you doing creeping into *my* compartment?"

"It's not *your* compartment; it's the *royal family's*. No one's allowed in here."

"*You're* in here." The girl cocked her head. "And I caught *you* creeping into the royal carriage without permission. You're gonna be in deep trouble."

"Yeah, well, you're going to jail!" Hal held out his hand. "Give me the brooch and the earrings, and I'll tell the police you came quietly."

The girl frowned. "What?"

"The jewels that you stole last night," Hal said, "from Mrs. Pickle and Lady Lansbury."

"There's been a theft?"

Hal nodded. "They're going to tell the police when we get to Balmoral."

"Ah nuts!" the girl cursed under her breath.

"It'll be much better for you if you give yourself up now."

The girl rolled her eyes. "I'm not a thief, you idiot."

"I'm not an idiot."

"You are if you think I'm a thief."

"Why are you hiding if you're not a thief?"

"I'm a stowaway."

"A what?" Hal faltered. He hadn't expected her to say that.

"I wasn't going to miss the Highland Falcon's last journey, but Dad said no children were allowed on the train." She looked at Hal accusingly. "Although that obviously isn't true."

51

"I wasn't supposed to be coming," Hal said. "My uncle brought me because my mom's in the hospital."

"Is she sick?"

"Yes . . . No. She's having a baby." Hal felt his chest get tight. He didn't want to talk about his mom. "You're a stowaway? How did you get on the train?"

The girl screwed up her eyes, regarding him with suspicion. "You have to promise not to tell."

"Tell who what?" Hal blinked. "I don't know anything."

"Dad would get into trouble. He could lose his job."

"The waitress who brought you food knows."

"Amy? Yeah, she's cool. She can keep a secret."

"I can keep a secret."

"Swear it. Say, 'I—' What's your name?"

"Harrison Beck."

"Say, 'I, Harrison Beck, swear with my breath and my spit never to tell anyone Lenny is on the Highland Falcon.'"

"Lenny?"

"It's short for Marlene." She leaned toward him. "You got a problem with it?"

Hal shook his head.

"Good. Right—say it."

"I, Harrison Beck, swear with my breath and my spit never to tell anyone Lenny is on the Highland Falcon."

Lenny spat on her hand and held it out for him to shake. He grimaced as the warm saliva rubbed between their palms, sealing the promise.

"My dad is the train driver," she said proudly, wiping her hand on her overalls. "Mohanjit Singh. The best steam engine driver in the country."

"Your dad's the driver?" Hal was impressed. "So he let you get on the train?"

"No! He'd never break the rules. The whole family drove up to Buckinghamshire, where the royal train is kept, to wave Dad off. After I hugged him goodbye on the footplate, I told Mom that he'd changed his mind and had said I could come. I hid in the tender on the way to London. When we got to King's Cross, I owned up." She grinned and jumped onto the bed, bouncing up and down. Her long black plait whipped about like a crazed snake. "I knew Dad'd have to let me come on the trip then. I couldn't go all the way back to Torquay on my own."

"Wasn't he angry?"

"A bit." She shrugged. "But he feels the same way about trains as I do—they're in our blood." Lenny dropped onto her bottom, and a toy mouse flew up out of the chest pocket of her overalls. She grabbed it and stuffed it back in.

"Is that a teddy?" Hal scoffed. "How old are you?"

"I'm twelve in three months." Lenny glared at him. "And it's not a teddy. It's Penny Mouse. Dad gave her to me the first time he let me ride on the footplate of the Highland Falcon. I thought she should come, too. How old are you?"

"I'm eleven." Hal sat down beside her. "And I've got a toy puppy called Pumu back home because I'm not allowed a real dog." He smiled sheepishly. "I didn't mean to laugh at your mouse. Can I see it?"

Lenny handed him the mouse. Its nose was a clump of black stitching gathered around horsehair whiskers, and it had a strip of black leather for a tail. "She lives in loco tenders and eats cheese. When I was little, I used to suck her tail."

"Gross." Hal passed it back.

"So tell me about this jewel thief," Lenny said, swinging her legs off the side of the bed.

Hal reached into his back pocket, took out his sketchbook, and pulled out the front page of Ernest White's newspaper. "Last night, someone stole Lydia Pickle's diamond brooch. Then, this morning at breakfast, Lady Lansbury said that someone had broken into her compartment and stolen her pearl earrings. I think this thief who's been stealing jewels from high-society parties"—he pointed at the article—"and the train thief are the same person."

"Whoa!" Lenny took the article. "It says here they stole a ruby ring right off someone's finger!"

"There's a reward for whoever catches the thief. It's ten thousand pounds."

Lenny shook her head. "That's not enough to buy a steam loco."

"You want to buy a train?"

"Not just any train. I want a streak—an A4 Pacific. Ten

thousand pounds wouldn't even get you the nameplate from a classic engine."

"You're odd."

"No—I love trains." Lenny looked at him. "Don't you?"

"I've never really thought about them." Hal looked about. "I suppose this one's quite cool."

"Quite cool?" Lenny looked disgusted. "You get to go on the final journey of one of the greatest trains ever built, on an A4 Pacific, the train that holds the world land-speed record for steam, and you think it is *quite cool*?" She shook her head. "There's something wrong with you." She jumped to her feet and grabbed his hand, pulling him up off the bed. "C'mon."

CHAPTER NINE

RAIL LEGS

Lenny checked the corridor was empty and darted out the door, pulling Hal behind her. Carpet was replaced by linoleum as they headed toward the front of the train. Hal could smell frying bacon, coffee, and engine oil.

"These are the service cars." Lenny let go of his hand as they passed cupboards, hatches, and shelves stacked with white towels and bed linens. "That's the pantry." She grinned at him over her shoulder. "Good for emergency cookies."

A horn suddenly blared, and the carriage lurched as an express train shot past them. Hal stumbled and whacked his elbow against the pantry door.

"Argh!" He grimaced as his arm fizzed like a thousand angry hornets. "Funny bone."

"*Shh*." Lenny put her finger to her lips.

"You didn't even wobble." Hal rubbed his elbow.

"Rail legs," she said knowingly. "It's like sea legs, but on trains."

"Is that a real thing?"

"Dunno." Lenny shrugged. "Bend your legs like you're standing on a skateboard. It helps."

Hal bent his knees and waddled after her.

"Not that much." Lenny giggled.

The corridor opened out into a compartment filled with storage boxes. A loading trolley was fixed to the wall beside two uniform jackets on hooks. A man in a blue suit and a cap with gold trim was seated on a wooden stool next to a switchboard, polishing a pair of shoes with a brush. Hal recognized him as the guard with the whistle from King's Cross. Lenny put her arm out, so that Hal stayed back.

"*Psst!* Graham," she whispered. "Close your eyes."

The train guard smiled, closing his eyes while continuing to polish the shoe.

"You haven't seen me," Lenny said in a whisper, waving at Hal to tiptoe with her across the carriage.

"I haven't seen anything." Graham chuckled. "I don't even know you're on board."

"Most of the train staff know I'm here," Lenny explained, as they marched on, "but Dad's asked them to turn a blind eye." She glanced at Hal. "I'm not supposed to talk to passengers, though." They passed a pair of compartments with three-tiered bunk beds closely stacked together. "And passengers are *definitely* not allowed in the service cars. The train staff don't like it. They work hard to give the passengers a magical experience, and a magician never reveals how they do their tricks." She pointed ahead. "That's where they go when they're off duty. They can't relax if passengers are bossing them about, asking for things."

Hal thought about the way Mr. Pickle had spoken to Gordon

Goulde, and how Lady Lansbury wandered around demanding things, and he completely understood.

The next carriage was an open space with two tables and benches. Amy was standing at a counter in the far corner, making a cup of tea with her back to them.

"Hi, Amy," Lenny said as they entered.

"What are you doing out of your room? You promised to stay hidden—" Amy turned around and went stiff. "Oh. Master Beck." She glared at Lenny, and Hal shifted uncomfortably from one foot to the other.

"Now, don't get mad!" Lenny said cheerfully. "Harrison found out where I was hiding. He said he wasn't sure whether he likes steam trains, so I'm going to take him to—"

"*Marlene.*" Amy's voice was serious. "This isn't a game. I could lose my job."

"I've sworn not to tell," Hal said. "I know I'm not allowed back here, but I promise to keep everything secret."

Amy sighed and turned back to the counter to add milk to her tea. "Your dad's shift started an hour ago."

"Thanks, Amy—you're the best."

"I'm a fool, is what I am," Amy said, more to herself than anyone else, as they scampered past her through a vestibule.

A door with a sign that read GENERATOR next to a yellow triangle with a black lightning bolt inside it was emitting an alarming electric hum. Beside it was a giant cage with a padlocked door and no windows, only a skylight in the roof.

"The luggage cage," said Lenny, hurrying past. "Your bags will be in there somewhere."

"I don't have bags," Hal replied, peering into the cage, stacked high with cases and carry-ons. "I only brought a rucksack. I wish Mom had helped me pack, though. I brought all the wrong stuff."

"Why didn't she?"

"One day, everything was normal; the next, I get told I'm going on a train with my uncle. Mom was too busy packing for the hospital to help me. I think they're worried about my baby sister."

"I've got three younger sisters. One time, when Nutan was born, I had to spend a whole afternoon with our next-door neighbor Mr. Tyrell. He's a bit strange. Doesn't go out during the day. Goes out at night to collect dead stuff for his taxidermy. But it turned out okay because he taught me how to skin a squirrel."

Hal grimaced. "I'd rather be on the Highland Falcon than skinning squirrels."

"I'd rather be on the Highland Falcon than anywhere else in the world." Lenny smiled. "Are you looking forward to being a big brother?"

"I don't know. I haven't thought about it."

"You don't think about much, do you?" Lenny laughed. "It's tough being the eldest. You get ignored. You have to share everything, and you're always told you've got to set an example."

"Like stowing away on a royal train?" Hal laughed.

"I'm serious." Lenny gave him a playful shove. "You'll see—everything will change once your sister arrives. She'll nag you to play with her all the time. Mine do, anyway."

"I'm not playing *girls'* games."

"What's a *girl's* game?"

Harrison shrugged. "Princesses?"

Lenny thumped him on the arm.

"Ow!"

"My sister Priya and I play princesses all the time. She makes me dress as a prince and fight her. Guess who wins?"

"You?" Hal's eyes flickered down to Lenny's tool belt.

"Priya, because she takes dance classes, so her legs are super-strong. She can take you down with a blow to the backs of your knees before you've swung a fist. She calls it combat ballet."

"Right." Hal nodded. "I'll remember to stay away from her, then."

Lenny laughed, grabbing the handle of the door at the end of the carriage and twisting the lock below it. She yanked it open. Hal was hit by a blast of cold air. His head rang at the clattering sound of the train traveling at speed. Facing him was the claret metal of the trough that held the coal. Lenny nimbly leaped over the gap between the carriage and the tender, opened a metal door, and disappeared inside.

Hal gripped an iron handle on the outside of the carriage and looked down. It was only a small jump. Railway sleepers rushed beneath him in a hypnotic blur.

Lenny's head popped back out of the metal door. "C'mon, slowpoke."

"I c-can't," Hal stammered.

"Imagine you're a ballet dancer!" Lenny shouted, disappearing again.

Taking a deep breath, Hal let go of the handle and jumped. He felt like he was falling but landed with a thump in the tender corridor, stumbling to his knees, his heart hammering in his chest as the roar of the locomotive shook the metal walls. He stood up on his feet unsteadily. It was dark, and the ceiling was low. The place stank of soot and smoke. As he stepped out onto the engine's footplate, wind whipped his hair back from his face. He gasped, overwhelmed by the vivid panorama of hedgerows, trees, and sky flying past the engine cab.

CHAPTER TEN

THE FOOTPLATE

Hal found Lenny standing beside the engine driver, who was leaning out of a glassless window, eyes on the track ahead. She grinned, yanking her dad's arm.

"Dad, this is my friend Harrison."

The engine driver turned. His head was covered with a navy turban, tied above a weathered forehead. He had kind brown eyes, and he was wearing blue overalls, like Lenny, with a light-blue shirt underneath.

"Friend? What friend?" He looked at Hal and frowned. "I told you to stay away from the guests, Lenny."

Lenny smiled at her dad sweetly. "He looked lonely."

"No, I didn't," Hal protested.

"He found my hiding place," Lenny admitted with a shrug.

The engine driver sighed. "Marlene Singh, you'll be the death of me." A warm smile broke out of his neat salt-and-pepper beard. "Good to meet you, Harrison. I'm Mohanjit Singh, father to the most disobedient girl ever to be born. And this"—he patted the shoulder of a man bent over behind him—"is Joey Bray, the Highland Falcon's fireman."

Joey Bray nodded at Hal as he thrust his shovel into the coal chute, turning and dropping the black rocks into the blazing furnace. Hal felt the heat against his cheeks and forehead.

"Lenny, love," her dad said. "I want you to sit in the fireman's chair while Joey's shoveling. And keep Harrison out of the way, too. We're about to take on water."

Springing across the footplate, Lenny pulled herself up onto the stool. "Isn't it *brilliant?*" she hissed at Hal.

Hal nodded. "Yeah," he said, pulling out his sketchbook and pen. He leaned on the metal of the cab to draw the spaghetti of silver tubes in front of him, as Lenny's dad pulled on a red lever.

"That's the regulator," Lenny said in his ear. "It controls the amount of steam going into the pistons."

"Coming up on the water trough in three miles," Lenny's dad said over his shoulder to Joey.

Joey nodded. "Righto."

Hal looked up at Lenny. "Can you drive this?"

She shook her head. "You have to have years of experience before you're allowed to drive a train like this one." She raised her voice. "And to be the driver of the royal train, you have to be the best engine driver in the world."

"It takes practice and teamwork," Lenny's dad said over the roar of the engine. "Joey builds a white-hot fire, evenly spread. Water from the tender travels over the fire in pipes, turning into steam, which is pushed down those pipes and bends back for a double heating. Reheated steam is more powerful. That steam is

Steam chest pressure gauge

Vacuum brake gauge

Fire box

driven down to a chamber at the front of the train with such great pressure, it pushes back the pistons, which turn the wheels."

"It's a blimmin' great kettle," said Joey, shoveling another load of coal into the furnace.

"Do you have to feed the fire all the time?" Hal asked.

"I shovel about a ton of coal every hour," said Joey, "but I ain't just dumping it in anyhow. You have to spread it about so the air passing through gets heated evenly."

"Joey gives her power, and I drive," said Lenny's dad. "This lever is the regulator, which makes the engine go faster or slower. And these are the brakes, if we need to slow her quickly. It takes a long length of track for a steam engine to stop dead." He tapped a gauge above Hal's head. "I have one eye on the pressure inside the boiler at all times, and I keep track of how much water is left in the tender so that we don't overheat and blow up."

"Steam engines blow up?"

Lenny's dad nodded. "If the pressure gets too high. But we

Main boiler
pressure gauge

don't let that happen. There are ways to let the steam out." He pointed at a chain in the middle of the tangle of hissing pipes. "Pull that."

Hal yanked the chain, and a high, jubilant musical note drowned out the chuffing of the engine for a moment as a jet of steam rushed out of the whistle. He looked at Lenny with delight and pulled the chain again.

Mr. Singh leaned out, then glanced at his watch. "The trough's coming up," he called to Joey.

The fireman nodded, knocking shut the furnace vent with the side of his shovel and passing the handle to Lenny. "Hold this, will you?"

Lenny took it, proudly, as Joey dusted off his hands and walked to the corner of the footplate.

"Half a mile!" Lenny's dad shouted to Joey.

Joey readied himself by a large crank in the corner, knees bent.

"Watch this, Hal!" Lenny's eyes were wide. "They're going to refill the tank. Look!"

She leaned out of the cab and pointed ahead. Hal looked down the streamlined nose of the claret engine as it huffed steam and smoke into the air.

"That's the tank where the water from the tender gets boiled into steam!" Lenny shouted. "Once the steam's pushed the pistons, it goes out the funnel. Gradually the water in the tender gets used up, and we have to refill it."

"You ready?" Mr. Singh cried.

"Aye!" Joey yelled.

Hal saw the rhythmic pattern of approaching railway sleepers change. Stretching ahead, between the rails, was a shimmering trough of water.

"DROP!" shouted Lenny's dad.

Joey furiously spun the giant crankshaft round and round with both hands. A loud splash and an earthquake of a roar came from underneath their feet. Torrents of water sluiced out from either side of the locomotive as if they were driving through a pond.

"Wahooooooo!" Lenny yelled into the wind.

Hal whirled around, trying to take everything in, his eyes wide and heart thundering. "What's happening?!"

"There's a big scoop underneath the tender." Lenny pointed down. "Joey lowers it with the crank as we drive over the water trough. The speed of the engine forces the water up into the tender." She pointed at the pressure gauge. "Look!"

Hal saw a needle rising steadily. Joey's eyes were glued to a pipe, which began to spit water into an overflow funnel.

"She's full!" Joey shouted, winding the crank han-dle the

other way to lift the scoop back up. The sound of gushing water subsided as the train chugged on, her belly full of water. Joey wiped his forehead on his sleeve, and Mr. Singh smiled.

"We just picked up three thousand gallons of water," said Lenny. "That's about twelve tons in ten seconds."

Hal looked at Lenny's dad and Joey in awe.

Joey winked and patted the engine. "She's a thirsty girl."

Lenny held out the shovel, and Joey returned to his rhythmic routine of delivering coal into the furnace.

"The Highland Falcon is *brilliant*!" Hal declared loudly.

Lenny grinned. "Told you."

"I don't understand. If the engine works so well, why are they getting rid of her?"

"She's old . . . and expensive to run." Mr. Singh looked out along the snaking track. "We need two crews for this journey. Daniel and Kerry, who did the night shift, are asleep. There are more-efficient engines now." He shook his head. "But none of them has the majesty of steam."

"But the Highland Falcon is *better* than normal trains," Hal said. "People should know about it. I'll bet everyone would want to go on a steam train if they knew how great they are. I mean, look how fast they go." He sniffed the air. "Is it me, or can anyone else smell baked beans?"

"Time for second breakfast," Joey said, reaching for a wrench. He jimmied three balls of silver foil from behind the pipes, knocking them onto his shovel. "These are piping hot," he said, tugging back the edges of the foil.

"Baked potatoes?" Hal said.

Lenny bent down by a small cupboard in the tender, taking

out three tin plates and laying them on the floor for Joey to put the potatoes on. The crispy parchment skins had split and were hissing and steaming. Hal's mouth watered as Lenny used a Swiss Army knife from her tool belt to score a deep cross in the top of each potato into which she pressed a chunk of butter.

Mr. Singh unscrewed a clamp, grabbed a rag, and—using it to protect his fingers—lifted down an open can of baked beans from the top of the boiler. The gloopy orange sauce inside bubbled and frothed. "The boiler gets up to fifteen hundred degrees," he said. "Pity to waste the heat."

Joey took a clean shovel from the cupboard, wiped it with a cloth, opened the furnace, and held it over the fire. Lenny passed him three eggs, which he cracked onto the shovel. They sizzled, their translucent innards turning white. A perfectly fried sunny egg landed beside the potatoes and beans on each plate.

"You can share mine," Lenny said, sitting down with her back against the tender. She pulled a fork out of her Swiss Army knife and offered it to Hal.

Hal sat down next to her, certain he'd never been so excited to eat a meal. He scooped potato and beans, dripping with egg yolk, into his mouth, gasping at the heat. It was the most delicious food he'd ever tasted.

"Now do you understand why I stowed away?" Lenny said.

Hal nodded, yolk dribbling down his chin.

Lenny beamed, taking the plate from him and leaning in. "So how are we going to catch this jewel thief, then?"

CHAPTER ELEVEN

THE MAGPIE

Having wolfed down his food, Hal watched with a smile as Lenny licked her plate clean.

"Have you got a list of suspects in that notebook of yours?" she asked him. "We should think about each passenger and their possible motives. That's what they do on TV."

"It's a sketchbook."

"Let's give the thief a name, like the Black Cat or the Pink Panther . . ." She tilted her head, thinking.

"What about the Magpie?" Hal suggested. "They like to steal sparkly things."

"That is actually brilliant." Lenny looked delighted. "Write that down in your book."

Hal pulled out his sketchbook and pen, turned to a blank page, and drew a magpie with a sparkling stone in its beak.

"Hey, you can draw." Lenny pulled the book from his hand. "Let me look."

"No, I—" Hal tried to grab it back, but she'd already turned the page.

"That's me!"

"Yeah." Hal looked at the footplate floorboards, his cheeks burning.

"No one's ever drawn me before." Lenny stuck her tongue out at the picture, mirroring the drawing. "It's good." She laughed and flicked forward.

"Who's this?"

Hal took his sketchbook back and closed it. "That's my mom."

"Oh, right . . ." Lenny changed the subject. "Think how brilliant it would be if we *did* solve the case."

"I might have to," Hal said. "Steven Pickle thinks I'm the thief."

"That overstuffed beet—what does he know?"

Hal suddenly realized he'd been gone from his room for a long time. "I should get back."

"I'll take you." Lenny stashed her dirty plate in the cupboard.

"Thank you for showing me the engine, Mr. Singh, and for the food, Mr. Bray. I've had the best time."

Lenny's dad shook his hand. "I would be grateful, Harrison, if you didn't mention to any of the passengers that you were on the footplate, or with my stowaway daughter. It may cause trouble."

Hal nodded. "You can count on me, Mr. Singh."

"Thank you." Mr. Singh smiled and turned back to his engine.

Lenny and Hal made their way back through the tender. This time, Hal barely felt a flicker of fear as he jumped into the carriage.

"Why is your uncle on the Highland Falcon?" Lenny asked, as they retraced their steps through the service cars.

"He's writing an article for the *Telegraph* about this journey. He writes a lot of books about traveling on trains."

Lenny stopped. "Is your uncle Nathaniel Bradshaw?"

Hal nodded.

"But he's my favorite writer! Have you read *Steam of the Dragon*?"

Hal shook his head. "I haven't read any of his books."

Lenny looked shocked.

"I'm going to," he added hastily.

"I'll bet he could help us catch the Magpie? He's probably noticing all sorts of clues."

Hal shook his head. "He doesn't believe there's a thief. He says no one would be mad enough to come on the royal train and steal things."

"Ha!" Lenny skipped forward. "Well, *we* know there's a thieving birdie on this train and we're going to catch it. We are train detectives."

"Lenny." Hal hurried after her. "How are we going to do that when you can't risk being seen?"

"You'll have to ask the questions and look for clues," she replied, frown lines appearing on her forehead. "Then you'll tell me what you've discovered, and we'll do the detective work together, 'cause I know this train inside out. Okay?"

"Okay."

"First, we need to know more about the stolen jewels. What

did they look like? Exactly when were they stolen and where from?"

"I didn't see Lady Lansbury's earrings. She said they were pearls. But I did see Lydia Pickle's brooch. Look, I'll draw it for you."

Hal sank to the floor, and Lenny knelt down beside him. Pulling out his sketchbook, he started to draw, but the jolting of the carriage jarred his pen. "Urgh, this is impossible."

"Put the book flat on the floor and lie on your belly," Lenny said. "Relax your arm and go with the motion of the train. Don't fight it."

Hal paused. "I think I know when the brooch was stolen."

"When?"

"You were there." He turned to a fresh page and drew five diagonal lines that would meet at a point if they continued off the page.

"What's that?"

Hal →

Lenny ←

"Perspective lines," he replied, half closing his eyes. He pictured the observation car, the groups of people standing and talking. Hal barely looked at the paper; his pen skittered about the page, drawing the scene.

"I was here," he muttered, "looking for you." He drew an *X*, and Lenny nodded. "Where *were* you, by the way?"

Lenny grinned. "Between the white cloth at the back of the trolley and Amy's legs."

"Then Uncle Nat came over, and as we left the carriage, Lydia Pickle complained about having lost her brooch." His pen went to her figure in the picture. "Yet here, only minutes earlier, it was pinned to her chest, because that's when I saw it."

Lenny stared down at Hal's drawing. "How do you do that?"

"Do what?"

"Draw that." She looked at him. "Like it's happening in front of you."

Hal shrugged. "If I tried to tell you what I saw with words, it would come out wrong. I get confused. I can't remember it right. But if I *draw* what I see in here"—he tapped his head with the pen—"it comes out right."

Lenny gave a quiet whistle. "With us on the case, the Magpie hasn't got a chance."

Hal felt a warm burst of pride. No one but his mom had ever been interested in his drawing.

They heard a noise, and Lenny quickly dragged Hal into the pantry. Looking through the slit in the door, Hal saw Graham the guard walk past.

"Come on! Let's get you back to your compartment before we get busted," Lenny hissed. "Let me see that drawing again." She

73

stared at the picture as they walked. "The Magpie must be one of the people in this picture. Wait—where's Ernest White?"

"There." Hal pointed to a circle. "That's the back of his head. He was seated in an armchair." His eyes flickered across the figures in the picture. He couldn't help noticing the person standing next to Lydia Pickle was Uncle Nat.

"We have to suspect everyone until we can prove they're innocent," Lenny said. "That's how these things are done on TV." She handed Hal's book back and slid open the connecting door to the royal carriage.

"As soon as I find anything out, I'll come and tell you," Hal said.

Lenny nodded. "And I'll see if the train staff know anything."

Hal hurried back, thrilled by their plan to catch the Magpie. His face felt tight from the wind and the heat of the furnace on the footplate, and he could still taste baked beans. As he rounded the corner, he could hear Mr. Pickle shouting.

"I demand you open this door!"

Uncle Nat was standing in the hallway, his back to the door of their compartment. Beside him was Gordon Goulde.

"I understand you're upset, sir," Gordon Goulde said, "but I'm afraid I can't do that. We respect our guests' privacy."

"Respect? That boy didn't show any respect for my wife when he bumped into us in the observation car and nicked her brooch!"

Hal winced. They were talking about him.

"The evidence we need to prove that boy is guilty is in there." Mr. Pickle pointed at the door.

"Then the police will find it when we get to Balmoral," Uncle Nat replied calmly.

"That'll give the boy time to hide the evidence or . . . or throw it out the window!" Mr. Pickle's round face was flushed, making him look like a salami. "There he is!" Mr. Pickle spluttered. "What are you smiling at, boy? Where have you been? I'll bet he's been stealing again."

"I'm not a thief," Hal said, feeling certain he hadn't been smiling.

"Check his pockets!" Mr. Pickle lurched toward him.

"Get your hands off my nephew." Uncle Nat leaped in front of Hal, pushing Mr. Pickle back.

"Mr. Pickle, *please*." Gordon Goulde grabbed Steven Pickle's shoulder, and the angry rail tycoon shrugged him off.

Baron Essenbach opened the door opposite Hal. "Is there a problem, gentlemen?"

"A small disagreement," Uncle Nat said in a steely voice. "Mr. Pickle seems to think he is Sherlock Holmes."

"What on earth is going on?" Sierra Knight stepped into the corridor clutching an electric-blue shawl around her shoulders.

Lucy Meadows was two steps behind her, holding what looked like a script.

"Would you mind keeping it down? I'm trying to run lines," Sierra Knight said.

"Open this door or—" Mr. Pickle started to say, but Uncle Nat interjected loudly.

"Gordon, I would like you to open up *Mr. Pickle's* room."

"What! Certainly not!" Mr. Pickle bellowed. "I'm the victim, not the thief!"

"I am sure if I made a thorough search of your compartment, I'd find your wife's brooch," Uncle Nat said, "as I suspect she has merely misplaced it."

"Outrageous!" Mr. Pickle's face was positively puce. "I will not allow you to root around in my private things."

"Precisely," Uncle Nat snapped. "Nor I you."

A cloud of barking white fur filled the far end of the corridor, followed by a grumpy-looking Rowan Buck. A few feet behind him glided a perfectly poised Lady Lansbury. The hallway was a traffic jam of people and barking dogs.

"Urgh, this is impossible!" Sierra grabbed Lucy by the wrist. "Come on. We're going to the observation car." And the two of them squeezed through the crowd.

Behind Lady Lansbury, Hal spotted Milo Essenbach enter the corridor. He had an odd look on his face, his eyebrows raised high.

Steven Pickle stepped aside to let Sierra pass, but the actress couldn't get past the excited dogs, who were suddenly barking and jumping up at her.

"Oh!" she wailed. "They're attacking me!"

"Hey, hey!" Hal rushed forward, kneeling before the dogs. "Sit!"

All five of the dogs immediately sat down, their curly tails wagging.

"Good dogs." Hal petted their heads, looking up at Sierra. "They're just being friendly."

Sierra looked uncertain, hurrying past the canines and toward Milo.

The baron's son shoved his hand into his pocket, bowing his head as Sierra and Lucy passed him. A flash caught Hal's eye. Something had sparkled between Milo's fingers.

It had looked a lot like jewelry.

CHAPTER TWELVE

THE INVENTION OF TIME

"So," Uncle Nat said, putting an arm around Hal's shoulder, steering him into their compartment, and closing the door, "where've you been?"

Hal sat on the sofa, noticing the beds had been put away. He wanted to tell the truth, but he wasn't about to break his promise to Lenny and her dad. He swallowed. "Nowhere."

"Ahhhh." Uncle Nat sat down in his desk chair. "Nowhere. Yes, I used to go there when I was a younger man." He smiled, but his eyes looked serious. "Hal, it would be better if you told me what you're up to."

"I can't!" Hal blurted out. "I promised."

Uncle Nat blinked, took off his glasses, and cleaned them with a cloth from the inside pocket of his jacket. "How about I tell you where I think you might have been, and you nod your head if I'm right?" He put his glasses back on and grinned. "That way, you wouldn't be breaking any promises."

Hal thought about this for a moment and then nodded.

"I noticed you entered the corridor from that direction." His uncle pointed. "That means you were either in the other carriage of compartments, the royal carriage, or the service cars . . ." He looked at Hal expectantly. "Or you could have been on the footplate."

Hal furrowed his brow, trying to stop a smile from spreading across his face.

"If you did happen to find someone kind enough to take you onto the footplate, then you would have witnessed the extraordinary event of the water scoop." He leaned toward Hal, his hazel eyes dancing, and Hal felt his own eyes must have been dancing, too.

He nodded the tiniest of nods.

"Oh, Hal!" Uncle Nat gasped, jumping to his feet. "Do you know how lucky you are? You've experienced something I never have . . . and probably never will. There are no water troughs in use anymore. They filled that one specially for this trip. I had my head and shoulders out the window trying to see it! And you were on the footplate?"

"It was amazing!" Hal exploded, bouncing up and down on the sofa. "Mr. Singh let me blow the whistle!"

"That was you?"

"Yes! And Joey gave me baked beans and potato cooked on the boiler." Hal's insides suddenly deflated as he realized he'd broken his promise to Lenny's dad. "But I promised I wouldn't tell."

"Listen"—Uncle Nat knelt down in front of him, holding up his right hand—"I, Nathaniel Peter Bradshaw, do solemnly swear that I will never tell a living soul that you have been on the footplate of the Highland Falcon, even though I'm jade with jealousy."

Hal smiled. "Thanks."

Uncle Nat hopped back into his chair, grabbing his pen. "Now, tell me all about it. It's priceless detail for my article. I couldn't see much out the window."

Hal felt a flutter of panic. He'd broken only half his promise. He mustn't betray Lenny. Changing the subject, he said, "Uncle Nat . . . um . . . I feel bad. I haven't read any of your books."

Uncle Nat blinked. "I can get you one, if you're interested."

"Mom told me about *Steam of the Dragon*. That sounds good."

"My adventure into China?" Uncle Nat put down his pen.

"Can I read it now?"

Uncle Nat stroked his chin. "We could see if the library has it."

"Good idea." Hal jumped up.

***

As they entered the library, a figure at the far end startled, dropping a leather-bound book to the floor.

"Apologies, Milo," Uncle Nat said. "We didn't mean to make you jump."

"It's fine." Milo picked up the fallen volume. "I was lost in thought."

Hal frowned. Ten minutes ago, Milo had been on his way back to his compartment. Why was he now in the library? He stared at the pocket he'd seen Milo put the sparkling object into, but the line of his trouser leg was flat. Whatever it was, it was gone.

"Hal is interested in my writing." Uncle Nat smiled down at Hal.

"I hear your uncle's books are superb"—Milo placed the fallen book on the shelf—"if you like trains."

"I do," Hal replied, realizing it was true.

"Right . . . I think I'll return to my room," Milo said to no one in particular and left.

The library felt and sounded different from the rest of the train. The walls of books deadened the sound of wheels on rails. There were no windows, but a soft light filtered in through three small skylights in the roof. There were two armchairs on either side of a green glass desk lamp perched on a square mahogany table in the middle of the floor.

Hal crossed the room to see which book Milo had been reading. He read the spine: *The Mating Call of the Mallard Duck*.

"Weird," he whispered to himself.

"Here we are." Uncle Nat put a pile of books on the table. "*A History of the World in Thirteen Railway Journeys*, *Sleeping Car to St. Petersburg*, *The Bishop's Branch Line*—which I wrote with the lovely Reverend James Challoner—and *The Invention of Time*."

"Where's *Steam of the Dragon*?"

"It appears to be missing." Uncle Nat looked pleased. "Someone must be reading it."

Hal picked up *The Invention of Time*. "How can someone invent time?"

"Not literally *invent* it. Before the railways came along, it wasn't important to be accurate about the time," Uncle Nat explained. "But, if you run a railway, you need a timetable. You have to be exact. The railways changed society in different ways, but in particular, how we measure and record time."

Hal blinked. "That's cool."

Uncle Nat's face lit up. "My books are travel stories, but they are also about how railways have changed the world. I have ridden the world's most extraordinary trains, from Stephenson's Rocket to the Japanese Shinkansen—"

The carriage jerked, and Hal stumbled as the Highland Falcon slid to a halt. "What's happening?"

Uncle Nat glanced at one of his watches. "It's ten thirty. We must be approaching Aberdeen." He stepped over to a framed map of the British Isles, which hung within one of the bookcases. "We're here." Uncle Nat ran his finger along a black line parallel with the east coast of Scotland. "We've crossed the Tay, passed through Dundee, and come up the coast." He looked at Hal. "At Aberdeen, the train turns around. Shall we go and see?"

Following his uncle out of the library, Hal saw a field of tangled rails, gray stones, and defiant thistles from the window.

"We're in Ferryhill Sidings." Uncle Nat went to the door at the end of the carriage. "Come on." He opened the door and jumped down to the track bed several feet below. "Be careful how you land on the ballast."

"Ballast?"

"The gray stones round the sleepers."

A salty summer wind buffeted Hal's cheeks, and he smiled as the stones crunched under his shoes.

"We've got to be quick to get a good view." Uncle Nat jogged alongside the train.

They picked their way over the rails to a low wall and sat down. A bird, which Hal recognized as a gray-backed barred warbler, burst out of a thicket of brambles and ivy, loudly trilling at them. Hal guessed her nest must be hidden in there.

81

Joey jumped down from the hissing engine and slipped between the tender buffers and the rest of the train.

"He's uncoupling the Highland Falcon from her carriages," Uncle Nat said.

Joey waved to Lenny's dad on the footplate, who eased the engine forward with two chugs of steam. Striding over the rails, Joey made his way to a tall iron lever beside the track.

"That changes the points," said Uncle Nat as Joey leaned into the lever. "Mohanjit can now reverse the loco along that parallel track, back this way."

Hal frowned. "Why aren't we going straight into Aberdeen?"

"The track doesn't loop round toward Ballater. We have to double back on ourselves and take a different line west. A train can't turn around, so instead the engine moves to the other end of the train. The Highland Falcon will pull us in reverse to Ballater."

"Will I be able to see the engine from the observation car?" Hal asked, watching Mr. Singh reverse the claret locomotive.

Uncle Nat nodded. "Mohanjit takes her up to the next set of points and then—"

His voice was drowned out by a great *shush* of water vapor as the Highland Falcon passed them, blasting steam from her whistle. They waved madly in reply. From the ground, Hal realized the enormous wheels were as tall as he was. He pulled out his sketchbook. He'd barely drawn the outline of the engine casing when he heard barking.

Lady Lansbury's dogs were bounding about in the scrubland beside the track. Rowan Buck followed them with a fistful of little black bags.

"I'd like to be a dog handler when I grow up," Hal said, watching Viking and Trafalgar play-fighting in the weeds.

"And spend your day picking up dog poo?" Uncle Nat laughed. "Mr. Buck doesn't look too happy to be doing it."

The Highland Falcon had huffed up the track, clanking over another set of points. Lenny's dad waited for them to shift and began to drive the loco forward, crawling toward the observation car. Hal continued to sketch, marking the outline of her claret belly and where her golden pipework became visible.

"Soon, we'll be chuffing through the River Dee valley," Uncle Nat said, standing by the observation car's buffers, watching Joey jog ahead of the engine.

"Does it take us to the castle?"

"It stops a few miles short, at Ballater. The royal family couldn't have a railway line running through their back garden."

A passing Inter-City Express honked its horn, and the Highland Falcon tooted her whistle in reply. Hal held up his picture, comparing it to the engine, and frowned when he caught sight of something white and fluffy moving between the wheels of the observation car.

It was Bailey.

"Closer . . . closer . . . ," Joey called, as the locomotive's giant wheels rolled toward the observation car.

Hal leaped to his feet in horror.

CHAPTER THIRTEEN

THE THRONE ROOM

"*Stop!*" Hal shouted, dropping his sketchbook as he sprinted forward, waving his arms madly.

Mr. Singh saw him and slammed on the brakes. Reaching the observation car, Hal dropped to his knees, panting, and scanned beneath the carriage. A pair of frightened blue eyes peered at him through the dark.

"Here, Bailey. C'mon, girl," he called to the dog.

Bailey made a whimpering sound, then bounded out from under the train, leaping into Hal's arms, knocking him to the ground and licking his face.

"S'all right, girl. I've got you."

"Is the dog okay?" Uncle Nat was holding Hal's sketchbook. He laughed as Bailey tried to sit on Hal. "I think she likes you."

"Bailey, you shouldn't play on the train tracks!" Hal scolded. "You could've been hurt."

Uncle Nat waved to Mohanjit and Joey to indicate the dog was okay. There was a high-pitched whistle, and Bailey shot out of Hal's lap. She ran to Rowan, who took two fingers from his mouth as the five dogs gathered at his feet, sitting on their haunches, tails wagging. He grimaced as he stooped to scoop a poo into a bag, which he dropped into another bag, before tying it up.

"He shouldn't have let Bailey run under the train." Hal scowled at the man. "She could have been killed."

Uncle Nat returned Hal's sketchbook. "I know. Come on—let's get back on board."

Hal followed his uncle up onto the observation car veranda and back inside. It was odd to see the iron face of the Highland Falcon peering in through the glass doors. She gave a cheerful whistle, a guff of black smoke pumping out of her funnel, as she hauled the train backward.

Steaming away from the main line onto a single track, they chuffed past the backs of people's homes. Hal watched as a girl ran to the end of her garden and excitedly waved at the train. The houses began to thin, alternating with flashes of green, until soon they were ambling through a verdant landscape.

"We're not going very fast," Hal said, thinking the River Dee looked like a silver ribbon threading through the valley.

"Special speed restriction on the royal branch line," Uncle Nat replied. He was seated in a leather armchair, scribbling in a small

pocketbook. "Queen Victoria never liked to go faster than thirty miles an hour."

"Can I go and get that book about inventing time from the library?"

Uncle Nat didn't look up but nodded.

***

The Invention of Time was lying just where they'd left it on the table. Hal picked it up, glancing up at the far door and wondering if he could get away with a quick trip to the royal carriage.

"*Psst!*"

Hal jumped. His heart startled into a canter as he looked around. The library was empty.

"*Psst!*"

He heard a familiar giggle.

"Lenny? Is that you?" he whispered. "Where are you?"

"Come to the history books."

Hal spotted a corner of books about the Tudors and made his way over. He brushed his fingers over the leather spines as he passed. One book sat out a little from the shelf: *The Tudor Beard Tax*. He instinctively pulled it, there was a *click*, and the case of books moved toward him. Behind the small secret door was a tiny chamber decorated with a mural of red and gold–leaf flowers. Inside, Lenny sat grinning up at him.

"Are you sitting on a toilet?"

"Shh." She grabbed him and pulled him into the bathroom, shutting the bookcase behind him. "This is not just *any* toilet," she said. "This is the *queen's* toilet!"

"The queen has a secret bathroom?"

"The queen doesn't *share* toilets," Lenny replied. "She is the only person allowed to . . . *you know what* . . . in here. And when she does, no one is allowed in the library."

"I'll bet she reads on the toilet." Hal chuckled. "Listen, I was coming to find you. I've got something to tell you."

"Me too." Lenny leaned forward. "I know who the Magpie is."

"What? I bet you don't."

Lenny lifted her nose. "It's Milo Essenbach."

Hal gasped. "How did you know?"

"I worked it out. Milo is the baron's *second* son." Lenny raised her eyebrows. "When his dad dies, he won't inherit a penny. In aristocratic families, the first son gets everything, and everyone else gets nothing."

"That doesn't seem fair."

"Apart from you and me, everyone on this train is rich or has been hired to do a job. They have no reason to steal jewels. But Milo Essenbach has a *motive*. He seems rich, but he's not."

Hal nodded. "And because he's a baron's son, he is surrounded by people with expensive jewelry."

Lenny smiled. "So he has opportunity . . . *And* he doesn't like trains. His dad is crazy about steam locomotives, but Amy says Milo looks bored when the baron talks about them. So *why* is he here?"

"To steal jewelry!" Hal grabbed Lenny's arm excitedly. "I saw something in his fist, something sparkly. He hid it in his pocket. And then he pretended to go off to his room, but ten minutes later, he was here in the library. Uncle Nat and I surprised him. He dropped his book and looked guilty."

"Which book was it? It might be a clue."

Hal shook his head. "It was just some dumb book about ducks."

"Oh." Lenny looked deflated.

"What should we do—tell the police?"

"We can't just accuse him. Who's going to believe a couple of kids? And I'm a stowaway, remember! We need proof." She frowned. "Has anything else gone missing since last night?"

"Not as far as I know." Hal shook his head, and an uncomfortable thought crept into it. "Lenny, what if Milo Essenbach didn't come on the Highland Falcon to steal small things like a brooch or earrings?"

"What d'you mean?"

"If I was a notorious jewel thief, I'd want to steal something big, from the richest people in the world . . ."

"The prince and princess!" Lenny's mouth dropped open, and she grabbed him. "I know what Milo's going to steal! The necklace that the prince gave his wife as a wedding present. It's from the royal collection. It's got the biggest flawless diamond in the world dangling from it. It's called the Atlas Diamond, and it's the size of a small egg. The newspapers say it's priceless."

"The size of an egg?" Hal tried to picture it. "How come you know about it?"

"Everyone knows about it! There were pictures on the front of every newspaper. A huge diamond on a chain studded with loads of smaller diamonds. She wore it at the wedding. *That's* what Milo's planning to steal—I know it!"

Hal felt a rush of urgency. "We have to stop him!"

"Or"—Lenny bit her lip—"we could try to catch him in the

act. Then we'd have the evidence we'd need to get him locked up and claim the reward."

Hal frowned. "But we don't know when, or how, he plans to steal it."

"Think about it. He can't steal the necklace until he meets the prince and princess. From the moment he says hello to Her Royal Highness at Balmoral, we won't take our eyes off him."

"When you say *we . . .*"

"Well, obviously *I* can't go to Balmoral. You'll have to do that."

Hal nodded. "And you could search his compartment while we're in the castle."

"I'll try." Lenny chewed her bottom lip. "But before the royal family gets on the train, there's always a security sweep. All train staff have to get off."

"Oh no! Won't you get caught?"

"When the train pulls into Ballater, I'm going to jump off before it stops. Dad says I have to tell Harold the stationmaster that I've stowed away." Lenny smiled. "He went to school with my dad. I'm going to stay with him till the train's ready to leave."

"If there's a security sweep, won't they find the missing jewels?"

"Only if they're looking for them, which they won't be. They'll be looking for bombs and stuff. Most of the train staff think Lady Lansbury is batty and has too much jewelry to know what she's lost . . . and that Lydia Pickle probably dropped her brooch, and it'll turn up."

"If I were Milo, I wouldn't risk leaving stolen jewels on the train," Hal said. "I'd bring them with me."

"Good point. Check his pockets."

"How am I supposed to do that?"

But before Lenny could answer, they heard Lydia Pickle squawk a greeting. Lenny put a finger to her lips.

"I just wanted to say—in private, like—that I trust you. I know you'd never nick my stuff."

"I'm sorry?" Hal recognized the honeyed voice of Sierra Knight right outside the door.

"You know, 'cause of what they said in *Hot Stories* mag—about how you was a bad girl come good."

"I was just a k-kid," Sierra stammered. "I would *never* steal . . ."

"Oh, I know. I just wanted you to know—now that we're mates—I never once thought you nicked it. Stevie thinks it's that boy, but I reckon one of them waitresses found it and kept it."

"Oh, right. Thanks. I'd appreciate it if you didn't mention . . . my past."

"Mum's the word."

"I'm . . . going to my room to get changed now."

"I'll walk with you."

Their voices drifted away.

"Oh, you don't have to."

"I want to."

Hal mouthed at Lenny, "*Sierra?*"

Lenny shook her head. "Too much to lose," she whispered. "It's Milo." She looked at her watch and put her ear to the door. "You should go—we're nearly at Ballater." She pushed Hal out into the empty library. "Remember: don't take your eyes off him."

Hal heard the train's whistle announce their approach to Ballater as he stumbled into his compartment. He grabbed the nice clothes and pulled them on, tucking his Saint Christopher into his shirt. Mom would laugh to see him dressed like this. He'd ask Isaac to take a photo to show her.

The brakes of the Highland Falcon hissed as they eased into the station. Hal leaned out the window. A small crowd of people were hanging over a fence by the quaint white station building, ogling the train. At the far end of the platform, he saw Lenny's dad jump down to shake the hand of the stationmaster.

Uncle Nat tapped him on the shoulder. "Oh good, you're dressed. Come here—let me redo that bow tie. There we are. Grab your blazer—it's nippy out there."

Ballater was a world away from King's Cross. Mountains framed the small town, and a crisp wind pushed Hal along the platform. He hurried forward, falling into step beside Milo, who was walking with Sierra and Lucy, his hands stuffed into the pockets of his gray coat.

"Honestly, Lucy, that Pickle woman is unbearable," Sierra muttered. "She won't leave me alone."

"I like her," Lucy replied. "What you see is what you get with her. It's refreshingly honest."

Milo said nothing as Hal followed the three of them through the station building and out onto the street, where four black Jaguars with tinted windows were parked. Hal gawked.

"Are they for us?"

Milo nodded. "I believe so."

Hal smiled at him, deciding he would try to get in the same car as his suspect, but Uncle Nat called him back to ride with him, Isaac, and Ernest.

Clambering into the car, Hal sat in the middle, leaning forward, his eyes glued to the car in front and the back of Milo's head.

CHAPTER FOURTEEN

BOWLED OVER AT BALMORAL

R ising from behind a wall of towering fir trees came the stone parapets of Balmoral. Hal felt as if he were in a movie as the convoy of black cars rolled soundlessly along the curved drive toward the castle.

"It looks like Camelot," he said, "but real."

"Fairy-tale architecture," Uncle Nat agreed.

The cars stopped in a neat line. The drivers got out and, like synchronized dancers, opened the doors for their passengers in unison.

Hal saw Sierra swing her legs out of the car in front, rising elegantly in her emerald pencil skirt and matching jacket with fur trim. Lucy Meadows climbed out after her, and Milo was the last to emerge.

"What are you waiting for, Hal?" Uncle Nat chided. "There's a prince and princess to meet."

Lady Lansbury had insisted on bringing her dogs. She got

out of her car, ignoring the driver's outstretched hand, and strode over to the baron. Behind her, Rowan struggled with the dogs, who were jumping around, yapping, and pulling in different directions, clearly excited to be outdoors again. Hal smiled, wondering if they were catching the scent of rabbits.

"The Scottish Highlands are truly magnificent," the baron declared to Lady Lansbury, audibly filling his lungs with fresh air.

Lady Lansbury raised her eyebrows and nodded. "Indeed."

Hal saw that Milo was standing apart from the group. Isaac screwed a long lens on to his camera and began taking pictures. Sierra pouted prettily for him.

An enormous pair of wooden doors swung open in the crenellated porch at the near corner of the castle, and out filed two rows of house staff dressed in black-and-white uniforms. The staff greeted the guests with silent bows and curtsies. Hal wasn't sure how to respond and found himself bobbing up and down as he walked past them. The prince and princess were standing in the doorway. The prince looked dapper, standing with his hands behind his back, wearing a suit with a tartan tie, a broad smile across his face. Beside him stood his wife in an ivory tea dress and a tangerine bolero embroidered with flowers.

The sun found a chink in the clouds and momentarily shone through dazzlingly bright, lighting up a sparkling stone the size of a bantam egg hanging around the princess's neck.

Hal gasped. It was the necklace Lenny had described. He looked over at Milo and noticed that he, too, was staring at the necklace.

Ignoring formalities, Sierra rushed toward the princess with her arms flung wide open. The two women greeted each other like sisters, squealing and hugging, then Sierra stepped back and did an elaborate curtsy, and the prince laughed.

"No! *Bailey!*" Rowan shouted. "Heel, boy. HEEL!" He lurched forward as the dog's leash flew from his hand.

Sierra cried out as Bailey bounded toward her. "Help! It's attacking me again!"

94

Rowan ran to grab Bailey's leash. The other dogs exploded free as he lost his grip on their leashes, and they all galloped toward Sierra, dragging their leashes behind them.

"Rowan!" Lady Lansbury snapped. "Get those dogs under control!"

Sierra screamed, but before the dogs reached her, the princess stepped in front of her and knelt down with her arms open wide, laughing with delight as the deluge of dogs bounced around her. She wrinkled her nose, closing her eyes as they licked her face.

"Viking! Bailey! Fitzroy! Get down!" Lady Lansbury rushed over to the princess. "Oh, Your Highness, I cannot apologize enough. Rowan!" She glared at her gentleman-in-waiting. "Get over here this instant!"

Hal wanted to help with the dogs, but he had just seen Milo slip into the porch. He watched as Lady Lansbury put an arm around the princess to keep the dogs at bay, bopping them on the nose with her purse.

"Naughty Trafalgar! I'm so sorry, Your Highness—they've been cooped up on the train all day. Get down, Shannon!"

"I don't mind!" The princess laughed as one of the dogs pushed its nose into her neck.

"My wife loves dogs," the prince explained to everyone proudly.

Taking his chance while everyone was distracted, Hal crept toward his suspect, doing his best to remain unseen. He could see Milo standing in the shadow of the porch, hunched over . . . examining something in his hand. Hal shuffled closer, trying to see what it was Milo was looking at. Suddenly there was a shout, and Hal turned to see Fitzroy running toward them, followed by a bellowing Rowan. Turning back, he caught sight of Milo stuffing a piece of paper into his coat pocket.

"Sit, Fitzroy," Hal said, and the dog did as he was told.

"Gotcha!" Rowan grabbed Fitzroy's leash and yanked the dog away so roughly, it whined.

Hal scowled at the man.

"I adore Samoyeds," the princess was saying to Lady Lansbury. "Such gorgeous creatures." She scratched behind Shannon's ears. "They always look like they're smiling." She turned to the prince. "I had one called Sammy when I was a girl. I loved that dog."

"They're normally so well behaved," said Lady Lansbury, covering her eyes with a gloved hand and shaking her head. "I can't think what's got into them. I truly am frightfully sorry."

"It's quite all right," said the prince, stepping forward and offering his arm to his wife.

"No, it is not." Lady Lansbury put up her hand in protest. "Rowan, take my babies back to the train *at once*. You can walk them to the station. They need the exercise."

Rowan's cheeks flushed. "But that's more than an hour's—"

"And this handbag you picked out for me"—Lady Lansbury turned her head away and held out her purse—"is all wrong. I shall luncheon without it." She slapped the clutch purse against his chest. "When we return to London," she added, "I'll be reviewing your employment contract."

With five leashes in one fist, and a lady's purse in the other, Rowan dragged the dogs away down the drive, all of them yapping and straining at their leashes, seemingly desperate to get back to the princess for one last cuddle.

"Shall we go in?" The prince motioned toward the castle.

"Your Highness"—Uncle Nat bowed his head—"I'm Nathaniel Bradshaw, and this is my nephew, Harrison Beck."

"Mr. Bradshaw"—the prince extended his hand—"it's a pleasure to meet you. My father is a huge admirer of railways. Your books are in all our libraries."

"Is it wonderful riding the Highland Falcon?" the princess said to Hal. "I can't wait to climb aboard."

Hal nodded, finding himself tongue-tied and unable to keep from staring at the enormous diamond dangling from her neck.

Uncle Nat nudged him gently. "Shake the prince's hand, Hal."

The prince smiled. "Correct me if I'm wrong, Master Beck, but your clothes look familiar."

Hal blushed as the prince shook his hand.

The prince winked. "Bet they're itchy."

Hal's mouth dropped open as Uncle Nat ushered him through the porch. He looked over his shoulder and saw the prince offer his hand to Ernest White and then embrace him like a friend.

"Oh, my days, she's wearing the *Atlas Diamond*!" Lydia Pickle whispered loudly to her husband. "That necklace is mint."

"Don't go getting any ideas," Steven Pickle grunted. "Just the cost of getting that rock insured would be enough to give me a heart attack."

Looking ahead for Milo, Hal realized with a horrible shock that he couldn't see him. He ducked under elbows and scanned the corridors, but there was no sign of him. He cursed himself for getting distracted. Lenny would not be impressed.

The housekeeper, a kind-looking woman with neatly pinned-back gray curls, ushered the group into a wood-paneled room as big as a village hall. It was carpeted with tartan rugs, and the heads of great stags were mounted on shields on the wall. The Pickles stood in the middle of the room loudly estimating the value of everything as waiters with trays handed out drinks. Sierra reclined on a chaise longue while Lucy sat awkwardly on a footstool at her feet. The baron stood before an enormous portrait of King Edward VII, but Milo Essenbach was nowhere to be seen.

"Would the young gentleman like a glass of orange juice?"

Hal nodded at the housekeeper. "Yes, please."

She turned to Uncle Nat. "I'm Gladys, sir." She bobbed her head. "Considering the lunch will be formal, we thought your nephew might prefer to eat in the kitchen with the other children?"

"That's a good idea," said Uncle Nat, looking at Hal. "Might be less stuffy and more fun. What do you think?"

"Um . . . uh . . ." Hal desperately tried to think of a good reason to stay. He needed to watch Milo, if the man ever returned. "But I like grown-ups."

Uncle Nat laughed. "Of course you do. Gladys, my nephew is being polite. He'd love to spend some time with people his own age. He's been trying to find someone to play with since we left King's Cross, but sadly there are no other children on the train." He looked at Hal. "Go and enjoy yourself."

"But—"

Before he could protest further, Gladys took a firm hold of Hal's hand and marched him out of the room.

CHAPTER FIFTEEN

BELOW STAIRS

As Hal descended a narrow flight of stone steps, the warm smell of baking bread greeted him. Gladys led him into a cavernous steam-filled kitchen with a range of stoves along one wall. Copper and silver pots and pans hung from ceiling hooks. A giant oak table in the middle of the floor was set with four places. A thickset boy who seemed about Hal's age was lowering a ladle into a pot bubbling away on the stove.

"Ivan!" Gladys snapped. "Get away from there. It's hot!"

"I'm hungry," Ivan complained, turning around and spotting Hal. "Who's he?"

"This is Harrison Beck. He's joining us for lunch today." Gladys pointed to two large sinks at the end of the kitchen. "You can wash your hands there, Harrison. Ivan, come and sit back at the table. Honestly, I can't leave you for a second."

"Nice bow tie," Ivan said with a disparaging snort.

Just then, a young girl ran in, wailing. Her pink satin dress was splattered with mud, and her carrot-colored ponytail disheveled.

"Melly! What has happened to you?" Gladys grabbed a cloth and rushed over to the girl.

"Oh, Gladys!" Melly sobbed. "I was coming through the flower garden, and a pack of white dogs attacked me."

"Attacked you?" Gladys said, aghast. "Did they hurt you? Did they bite you?" She turned the girl around, looking for injuries.

Melly sniffed. "They knocked me over and licked me!"

"They wouldn't hurt you," Hal said, drying his hands. "They're friendly dogs—just puppies, really."

Melly scowled at him. "Are they *your* dogs?"

"No." Hal took a seat at the table. "They belong to Lady Lansbury, but I met them on the Highland Falcon."

"Melly." Gladys's voice was stern as she took the girl by the shoulders. "What's that I can smell? Have you been in the princess's room again?"

"No." Melly's blue eyes grew wide. She was obviously lying.

"How many times have I told you not to play with her things?"

Melly's bottom lip trembled. "I just did a tiny squirt of her perfume."

"If I find out you've been going into her room without permission," Gladys said, steering Melly toward the table, "I'm going to tell your mother."

"So, you've been riding on the Highland Falcon?" Ivan said, turning to Hal and grabbing a roll from a basket in the center of the table.

Hal nodded enthusiastically. "It's the most incredible train—"

"Only nerds like trains," Ivan interrupted flatly.

"If you'd seen the royal train, you wouldn't be saying that," Gladys scolded, placing a casserole dish on the table. "It's

beautiful." She picked up the ladle. "Now, who wants some
of Cook's sausage-and-apple casserole with mashed potatoes?"

They all nodded, and she began to fill their plates.

"Ivan, will you look after Hal?" Gladys wiped her hands on a
tea towel. "I have to pop upstairs to help with the lunch service."

Ivan burped loudly and grinned nastily at Hal. "Yes, Gladys,"
he said sweetly.

"I shan't be long." As she bustled out of the kitchen, she called
over her shoulder, "There's trifle in the fridge for dessert."

There was an awkward silence. Then Ivan began to slurp up
his casserole loudly. Melly looked at him with disgust.

"It must be pretty cool, living in a castle," Hal said.

"It is," Ivan replied. "My dad's the head butler. He's the boss of
this place. I can go wherever I want. Nobody tells *me* what to do."

"He isn't the boss," Melly scoffed.

"I know places in this castle even my dad doesn't know about,"
Ivan boasted. "I have a map of the secret passages. Sometimes, I
spy on the queen."

"No, you don't!" Melly rolled her eyes and looked at Hal. "My mother is a lady-in-waiting. No one spies on the queen, and there are no secret passages."

"Are too."

"Could you show me?" Hal said, suddenly getting an idea. "I'd like to see."

Ivan ignored Hal. "Who's up for trifle?" He pushed his chair back from the table and walked over to the fridge, taking out a dessert bowl. He brought it to the table and spooned out an enormous portion for himself.

"Seriously, if it's true that you can go anywhere you want," Hal said, seizing his chance, "why don't you prove it?"

Ivan raised an eyebrow, filling his mouth with jelly and custard. "What if I don't want to?" he mumbled.

Hal smiled. "Then I'll know you're talking rubbish," he said, crossing his arms.

"C'mon, then," Ivan said, pushing his chair back. "You'll see."

Hal followed Ivan upstairs. They walked down a corridor lined with paintings of Scottish mountains, and Hal caught the murmur of voices and the clinking of crockery. He wanted a peep at the grown-ups eating their lunch. He had to know whether Milo was with them. But before they reached the dining room, a smartly dressed attendant stepped out from a doorway and held up his hand.

"Ivan," he said sternly, "what're you doing here?"

"Hi, Alec," Ivan replied brightly. "I'm showing Harrison around the castle."

Alec gave Ivan a suspicious look. "Aye, and what else might

you be up to? We both know what kind of trouble you like to get into."

"Hal said he wanted a tour of the castle, and seeing how he's a guest, I'm giving him one." Ivan's face was a picture of innocence.

"Well, take a wee tour in the other direction"—Alec twirled a white-gloved finger—"because I'll not be letting you anywhere near the royal party."

"Fine," Ivan replied, spinning on his heel. "C'mon," he said to Hal. "We'll go this way."

They passed through a door and into a room that looked out over a garden of box hedges.

"Thought you could go wherever you wanted." Hal couldn't help smiling.

"Shut it."

"So where are these secret passages, then?"

"There's one over here." Ivan walked over to a window, dragging a tall-backed chair with him. "Come see."

Curious, Hal followed him.

"Get up on the chair and run your hand along the top of the window," Ivan said.

Hal climbed up and had to rise onto his toes to reach the top of the window.

"There's a lever," Ivan said. "Can you feel it?"

Hal strained to stand as tall as possible and felt along the wooden frame with his fingertips, but he couldn't find anything. He heard a clunk, then felt a hand shove him hard. He fell forward, out through the now-open window. He landed face-first in a flower bed, his chin sinking into cold, damp earth. He spat out soil. Suddenly, from above, there was a loud bang. Hal looked up.

Ivan had shut the window and was waving and grinning down at him.

Getting to his feet, Hal tried to look as if being shoved out a window hadn't hurt. He put his hands in his pockets and strolled off, trying not to limp. His knees were wet with mud from the flower bed. For the first time since he'd put it on, he was glad of the itchy blazer. He sank his chin down and hugged his arms against his sides to stop from shivering. The wind was cold. Hurrying around the corner, Hal searched for a way back into the castle. A gust of wind brought him the bombastic bass of Mr. Pickle's voice, and there was Sierra's tinkling laugh. Ahead of him, a bay window glowed yellow. It appeared as though the condensation on the inside of the glass had prompted someone to open the top casements.

Hal snuck up and stepped into the flower bed, peeping into the dining room. It wasn't as grand as he'd imagined. He saw a granite fireplace, and above it an enormous mirror stretching up to a crenellated cornice. The prince sat at one end of an oval dining table, sandwiched between Lady Lansbury and Lydia Pickle. The princess was at the other end, seated between Uncle Nat and Milo Essenbach. Hal was relieved to see the Atlas Diamond still hung about her neck, although alarmed that Milo had managed to get himself a seat right next to it.

Pulling out his sketchbook, he drew the table, marking where each person was sitting.

A man, who Hal assumed could only be Ivan's father, dressed in black and looking every bit as disagreeable as his son, was standing by a mahogany cabinet, surveying the room and making silent but aggressive gestures to the serving staff. Hal immediately

104

realized no one would be able to steal the princess's necklace under his watchful eye.

"That's the trouble with these old castles and country houses," Steven Pickle was saying to the baron. "Expensive to run. There's the maintenance and the staff, and I don't want to even think about the insurance. *Sheesh!*"

Ernest White seemed very uncomfortable to have found himself seated at a royal table and kept trying to help the waitstaff. At the other end of the table, the princess was teasing Milo about being a bachelor.

"You can't put off marriage forever."

Sierra giggled. "I keep telling him that."

Milo smiled awkwardly. Hal focused on Milo's face, flipped the page, and drew the snarling lip and angry forehead lines that pinched his dark eyes together. He looked every bit the criminal.

Meanwhile, Lady Lansbury was talking to the prince about horses, and he was nodding, but Hal noticed his eyes flicker to the end of the table every few seconds to look at his beautiful wife.

Hal turned another page, and his pen darted across the

paper, getting down the lines of Lady Lansbury's profile and the distracted face of the prince—more impressions than actual drawings.

A sudden pain stung the back of his head. Hal looked about, trying to work out what had hurt him. Was it a wasp or a bee? He felt another hot shock of pain on his wrist, and then another on his cheek.

On the ground, he saw a ball of chewed-up paper. And then a hail of them began to hit him in quick succession. He shrank back against the wall and looked up. There, up in a turret, he saw Ivan, leaning out of a window with a straw.

"Nerd!" he shouted.

Cursing Ivan under his breath, Hal leaped onto the path and jogged away as spots of rain hit him. There was a red mark on the back of his wrist where Ivan had shot a pellet at him. He shoved his sketchbook into his blazer pocket and broke into a sprint as the rain got heavier. He turned a corner, then another and another. In the distance, he could see the porch where they had entered Balmoral.

Lifting the iron ring, Hal was relieved to find that the porch door opened. He stepped inside and shook himself like a dog. He was soaked. Looking down, he saw his knees and shins were caked in mud. A raindrop dripped off the end of his nose. He looked about for something to use as a cloth . . . and there it was: Milo Essenbach's graphite-gray woolen coat—the one he'd been wearing earlier when Hal had seen him stuff that mysterious piece of paper into his pocket.

It was hanging right in front of him on the wall-mounted coatrack.

CHAPTER SIXTEEN

SECRETS AND SCONES

Going through someone's pockets was wrong. But so was stealing jewels. What if the brooch and earrings were in those pockets? Hal took a deep breath and plunged his hands into them. His left hand pulled out a packet of tissues. His right, a crumpled piece of paper. He unfurled the note.

> People are getting suspicious – you must be more careful, or we will be caught. Stick to the plan. We can have everything we dreamed of if you keep calm and stay out of sight. Once we are safely off the train in London, no one can stop us.

Milo had an accomplice! Pulling out his sketchbook, Hal hurriedly copied down the note to show Lenny. The Magpie was not one person but two! *One for sorrow, two for joy . . .*

"What are you doing?"

"Gahhhhh!" Hal yelled, dropping his pen as he spun around. Melly was standing a few feet away, watching him.

"What am *I* doing?" he almost shouted. "What are *you* doing creeping up on me? You frightened me half to death!"

"I came to find you. I thought Ivan might have played one of his mean tricks."

"He did," Hal said, bending down to pick up his pen. "He shoved me out a window and shot pellets of paper at me." He pointed to the welt on his wrist. "I'm covered in mud and soaked through."

"Could've been worse," Melly said with a half smile. "He locked my cousin in the pig shed. The pigs thought she was food." She moved toward Hal, trying to look at his sketchbook. "What were you doing going through the pockets of that coat?"

"I can't tell you," he said, snapping his book shut. "You're too young."

"I'm seven and a half." She cocked her head. "And you looked like you were stealing."

"I wasn't! Look—if I tell you, you can't tell anyone else."

Melly nodded. "Promise."

"I was doing detective work." Hal crumpled up the note, dropping it back into Milo's coat pocket. "Very important, secret detective work."

"Detecting what?" She was suddenly so close she was almost stepping on his toes. "You can trust me. A lady-in-waiting has to be good at keeping secrets."

"A lady-in-waiting?"

"That's what I'm going to be when I grow up, like my mom."

"Right." Hal smiled. "I bet you'll be brilliant at it."

"You're nice." Melly beamed. "I can help you with your detecting if you like. What's the crime?"

"It hasn't happened yet, but we think one of the guests on the train plans to steal the princess's diamond necklace."

"The Atlas Diamond?" Melly shook her head, her ponytail flicking from side to side. "That's impossible. The princess has a guard who watches the necklace the whole time she's wearing it. His name is Hadrian, and he's ginormous, like a giant."

"What about when she takes it off?"

"She puts the Atlas Diamond in a special metal case with a number lock and gives the case to Hadrian. He handcuffs it to his wrist—"

"There you are, Hal!" Gladys sang out, clapping her hands together as she rushed toward them. "It's time to get you back to that train, young man. Thank you, Melly, for, er . . ." She looked quizzically at Hal's muddy trousers. "Looking after our guest."

"That's okay. Bye, Harrison." Melly hugged him, whispering, "I hope you solve the case."

Hal hugged her back. "Bye, Melly . . . and thank you."

***

"What on earth have you been up to?" Uncle Nat exclaimed, staring at Hal as he came down the hallway. "You look like a rat that went for a swim in a hippopotamus's hollow and almost drowned."

"Um, well, you see, um . . ."

"Let me guess, you've been *nowhere*, getting up to *nothing*?" Uncle Nat's eyes twinkled.

Hal grinned. "Kind of."

"You can fill me in when we're back on the train."

Hal nodded gratefully and moved toward the door, but his uncle put a hand on his shoulder. "We leave the premises in order of social standing."

"What does that mean?"

"We go last because we don't have a title. We're *nobodies*, remember?" Uncle Nat waggled his eyebrows.

The prince and princess walked outside through the door, followed by Lady Lansbury on the arm of the baron, then Milo Essenbach. The black cars were lined up on the gravel. There were six now. Standing beside the prince and princess's vehicle was the biggest man Hal had ever seen. He had shoulders like a bison and was a head taller than the other men. *Hadrian*, Hal thought.

Since they had left, a host of volunteers had clearly been busy decorating Ballater station for the royal departure. The Highland Falcon was in her proper formation—her gleaming locomotive at the front, ready to pull her carriages back along the line to Aberdeen—and hundreds of people lined the road outside, waving Union Jacks.

"Wow." Hal stared out the window at the happy faces.

"This is the first time the branch line has been used since the museum reopened," Uncle Nat said. "Tragically, the original station burned down a few years back, so today is a cause for celebration."

Their car stopped beside a red carpet that led through the station to the platform, and they all got out. Hal blushed as people cheered. He hoped no one was looking at his muddy knees.

The prince and the princess were in the last car. Hal was getting on the train when he heard the crowds go wild.

"I should stay and watch," Uncle Nat said, as the prince shook hands with a pensioner, and a girl stumbled forward with a bouquet for the princess. "But you should probably go and change your clothes."

Stepping through the door of their compartment was a relief. Hal pulled the blinds down and quickly got into jeans and the maroon-and-navy sweater his mom had knitted for him. As he sat down on the floor to pull on his sneakers, he found a piece of paper in one of his shoes.

He took his sketchbook from the blazer pocket and tucked the paper inside. The note had to be from Lenny.

Uncle Nat came in and sank onto the sofa. "I don't know how they do it, all that smiling—and after such a big lunch. I don't think I'll eat for days."

Hal looked up. "Where is Birsemore station?"

"It's a few stops along the line," his uncle replied, getting comfy. "About half an hour away. We won't be stopping, though. Now that the prince and princess are on board, the train will slow down through every station so they can wave to the crowds."

"Would you mind if I ordered scones?"

"Didn't Gladys feed you?"

"Yes . . . I, er, thought I might be hungry again in half an hour."

"Go ahead." Uncle Nat shook his head in wonder. "You must have hollow legs." He closed his eyes. "I think I'll let my thoughts percolate, maybe write up today's activities later." His breathing became heavy. "Say something to Gordon about those trousers, won't you?"

A minute later, Uncle Nat was making snoring noises.

Hal pressed the intercom buzzer.

"Hello? How may I help you?" Amy's voice crackled through the speaker.

"I'd like scones at Birsemore station," Hal said in a low voice. "This is Harrison—Harrison Beck."

"Perhaps sir would like to eat the scones in the gentlemen's lounge?"

"Er, yes, I would. Thank you." He let go of the button.

Hal dashed to the observation car to see the prince and princess greeting the crowds. Soon they were done, and the Highland

Falcon blew her whistle, and she steamed out of Ballater station with the crowds cheering. Isaac was out on the veranda, snapping pictures of the waving onlookers on either side of the tracks. Hal stood beside the photographer, watching the rails spooling out behind them as Balmoral disappeared.

"Shut those doors," Milo growled from a leather armchair. "It's freezing in here."

Apologizing as he came back inside, Hal wondered if the sight of Hadrian had upset Milo. He chose a seat in the corner and took out his sketchbook. Hal looked down at the words he had copied down from Milo's letter and wondered who his accomplice might be. Sierra Knight, maybe? He needed to speak with Lenny urgently!

As the train rumbled back toward Aberdeen, Hal's pen turned a fresh blank page into a picture of Balmoral.

He silently thanked Queen Victoria for the speed restriction. It was much easier to draw when the train traveled slowly.

***

On the approach to Birsemore, Hal made his way back through the train, passing Ernest White and the baron playing billiards. Lucy was in the library reading a book. With a jolt, Hal saw it was *Steam of the Dragon*, but he didn't have time to stop now. The Highland Falcon was slowing to a crawl, and waving crowds were visible from the window.

Lady Lansbury was playing solitaire with a deck of cards in the gentlemen's lounge. Hal entered the room and took a seat at a table on the opposite side of the carriage and turned away from her, looking out the window next to him.

Amy arrived with a tray held against her shoulder. She placed a plate of two scones, a pot of strawberry jam, and a dish of clotted cream on the table in front of Hal's armchair. Then she lifted down an old-fashioned cream telephone with a gold rotary dial, plugged the cable into a socket in the wall, and winked at him.

Rowan entered the carriage as Amy left, sitting down opposite Lady Lansbury.

"Did you take the dogs to the toilet before the train left?" Lady Lansbury asked coldly.

"I did." Rowan nodded. "All bagged and labeled."

"Good. And did you feed them?"

Rowan shot a sideways glance at Hal. "Not yet."

"What do you mean, *not yet?*" Lady Lansbury demanded in an angry whisper. "For goodness' sake, do it at once!" She paused, then said loudly, "The poor dears must be starving."

Hal cut his scones in half and smeared jam across them. A small red light on the telephone flashed at him. He put down the knife and picked up the receiver. "Hello?"

"It's me," said Lenny's voice.

"Where are you?" he whispered into the phone.

"I'm in the generator room, at the front of the train."

"Where?"

"Near the luggage cage. Remember? Come and find me—and bring the scones."

"But I can't . . . Hello? Lenny?"

The line was dead.

Hal replaced the receiver and glanced across the carriage. Lady Lansbury was on her own again. Quickly adding cream to the scones, he gathered them into a napkin. The generator room was behind the door that buzzed with a yellow triangle sign split by lightning. It was dangerous. And how was he going to get to the other end of the train? He'd have to go through the royal carriage, which was now occupied and guarded. He got up with his parcel of scones and announced, "I think I will go and eat these in my room."

CHAPTER SEVENTEEN

THE ELECTRIC NEST

Walking through the train with his scones, Hal agonized over a good reason for having to pass through the royal carriage. He reached the forbidding door, took a deep breath, and knocked.

"Excuse me, sir," he said to the beefy man in a navy-blue suit who opened it. "I know I'm not allowed through here, but the train guard, Graham . . . Have you met him? He's ever so kind . . . Well, it's his birthday"—Hal could hear himself gabbling—"and I've got some scones for him, as a present." He held up the napkin. "And I was hoping you'd let me pass through to give them to him? I want to sing him 'Happy Birthday.'" He smiled his politest smile. "You can search me or escort me, if you like?"

The guard chuckled and waved him through, putting a finger to his lips.

Hal gratefully scurried through the living room to the corridor. Hadrian was standing guard in front of the prince and princess's compartment, where Hal had first discovered Lenny.

116

The bodyguard looked even bigger indoors because he had to stoop to prevent his head from hitting the ceiling. Hal's heart pounded as he walked past, smiling at the man, who replied with a piercing look.

Stepping into the service car, Hal closed the door behind him and collapsed against it with relief. Once he'd caught his breath, he darted through the crew's mess to the door with the yellow triangle on it and knocked. The door opened, and a hand shot out, grabbed his wrist, and pulled him inside.

"Well?" Lenny demanded, grabbing the scones. "What happened? Did he try to steal it? What's Balmoral like? Did you see the necklace?"

The generator room was hot, dark, and stank of diesel. An unnerving buzzing noise came from a giant metal unit covered in blinking lights and sprouting cables of many colors. On the floor in front of it, Lenny had made a nest from old towels and tablecloths.

"Is it safe in here?"

"'Course it is, as long as you don't touch the generator. C'mon—sit down. I want to hear what happened."

"Nothing happened, but—"

"Nothing?" Lenny looked appalled. "Are you sure?"

"Let me finish. When we arrived at Balmoral, I was sent to eat in the kitchen with the castle children, but I tricked this boy called Ivan into taking me outside so I could watch the adults through the window."

"That was clever."

Hal felt himself blushing at the lie. "The princess was wearing the necklace the whole time."

"You saw it? What's the Atlas Diamond like?"

"Big and sparkly?"

Lenny rolled her eyes, and he shrugged.

"Milo sat next to the princess at lunch, but he couldn't pinch it—there were too many people watching. And I'm not sure he's going to be able to steal it at all, because there's this giant guard called Hadrian who never lets it out of his sight."

"But Milo must have known the necklace would be guarded."

"There's more." Hal paused. "I found something . . ." He was enjoying the look of intrigue on Lenny's face. "I ran around to the front of the castle, to the porch, where all the coats were hanging."

Lenny sat up on her knees. "You didn't?"

Hal nodded. "I searched his coat pockets."

"*And?*"

"There was a note."

"Did you read it? What did it say?"

Pulling out his book, Hal turned to the page where he'd copied down the note and passed it to Lenny.

"He has an *accomplice*," said Lenny breathlessly.

"Of course!" She shoved half a scone smothered in jam into her mouth. "That's how he's going to do it."

"But you should see how heavily it's guarded. When the princess wears it, Hadrian follows her like a shadow. And when she takes it off, it gets locked in a metal briefcase and handcuffed to Hadrian's wrist."

"If Milo *does* steal the necklace, I'll be impressed," Lenny said, spraying scone crumbs everywhere.

"The note says *stick to the plan*"—Hal tapped the sketchbook—"so they must *think* they can steal it."

"Maybe the guard's in on it?" said Lenny, taking Hal's book and flicking through it. "Or maybe they're going to snatch it and not care who sees?"

"You know what I've been thinking?" Hal said. "A brooch is like a badge. It's pinned to your clothes."

"Yeah—so?"

"It would be hard to steal one without someone noticing. You'd have to have quick fingers."

"Or Mrs. Pickle would have to be as thick as porridge," Lenny said. "Which she is."

"I'm not so sure." Hal frowned.

Lenny came to Milo's portrait and stared at Hal's drawing. "That scar. He looks like a jewel thief."

"He was acting weird at Balmoral. When there was a kerfuffle with the dogs, everyone rushed forward except for Milo. He slunk right back against the porch and then disappeared."

"What kerfuffle?"

"Rowan lost control of the dogs, and they knocked the princess over," said Hal. "He's a terrible dog handler. Lady Lansbury was furious—she embarrassed him in front of everyone. But d'you know, I noticed something odd—Rowan called Bailey a boy, and Lady Lansbury got all their names wrong. If they were my dogs, I'd never get their names wrong."

"Yeah, but you love dogs!" Lenny held up the double page of dog sketches Hal had done.

"True." Hal laughed. "So what are we going to do?"

"The royal tour officially kicks off when we get to Aberdeen. You can bet the princess will be wearing the famous necklace. People want to see it."

"You think that's when the Magpie will strike?"

"Yes. The accomplice's job will be to distract Hadrian," Lenny said. "Create a diversion."

"Who do you think the accomplice is?" Hal asked.

"It could be Sierra. She's always whispering in his ear."

"That's what I was thinking."

Lenny nodded. "You must stay close to the necklace. Don't let anything distract you from watching it." The carriage tilted and slowed. She checked her watch. "We're back at Ferryhill Sidings—you should go."

Turning on his heel, Hal dashed through the service cars, then slowed and walked timidly into the royal carriage. He saw Hadrian bow and step aside as the prince and princess emerged from their compartment. The princess had changed into an emerald-green dress, but she was still wearing the Atlas Diamond, as Lenny had said she would. He followed the royal party at a discreet distance to the observation car, as the train rumbled into Aberdeen station.

Cheering crowds were packed six or seven deep along the platform. Hal felt a bubbling up of joy as he watched the awe on the faces of people seeing the Highland Falcon for the first time. He realized how lucky he was to be on this train. He looked about for his uncle and spotted him chatting with Ernest White.

"Uncle Nat," Hal said, crossing the carriage, "I didn't say it before, but thank you for bringing me on the Highland Falcon." He felt a blush creep up his cheeks. "It's pretty cool."

A smile stretched across his uncle's face. "See, Ernest—I'll make a chuffer nutter out of him yet." His amber eyes danced. "I'm glad you're enjoying yourself, Hal."

Hal nodded. "I am."

Isaac was already working, taking pictures. The princess was with Sierra beside the door to the veranda. She fanned herself with her hand and turned to Sierra.

"Do you have perfume in your purse?"

"Always." Sierra took an octagonal bottle from her handbag.

"Gyastara—that's my favorite."

"Mine, too." Sierra spritzed the princess's neck.

"How do I look?" The princess appeared nervous.

"You're perfect."

The distant *parps* of a brass band got louder as the train crawled along the platform. The princess turned, catching Hal staring at her. "It's exciting, isn't it?" she said.

"Aren't you worried about wearing your necklace?" Hal blurted out exactly what he was thinking. "What if it's stolen?"

121

"I don't have to worry. Hadrian takes care of everything for me." She pointed over Hal's shoulder, and he turned to find Hadrian standing right behind him. She cupped her mouth with a hand and whispered, "It gets a bit heavy, though."

"Oh." Hal was unsure what to say, and the princess giggled.

The other train guests were in the carriage now. Milo was propped against the bar, on his own. The Highland Falcon came to a halt, releasing a cloud of steam, and the prince and princess stepped out onto the veranda. The crowd roared with delight, and Hal couldn't help smiling. The royal couple were helped onto the platform by an attendant, who introduced them to a beaming man in a black suit with an enormous gold chain and medallion around his neck.

"The Lord Mayor of Aberdeen," Uncle Nat said, scribbling in his pocket book.

"Are we getting off?" Hal asked, his eyes following the necklace.

"No. The royal couple will exchange a few pleasantries, Isaac will take a few pictures, and then we'll be on our way on the first leg of the royal tour." He looked at Hal. "This evening, there'll be a feast to celebrate, and everyone has to wear their best clothes."

"But my trousers are muddy," Hal replied, panicking as he realized he'd forgotten to ask Gordon to clean them. "Can I wear my jeans?"

"No. No jeans." Uncle Nat shook his head. "Don't worry— Gordon said he has tartan trousers that match the blazer. We can borrow those."

Hal gasped with horror. "Tartan trousers!"

Uncle Nat burst out laughing.

"Are you joking?"

"You should have seen your face!" Uncle Nat hooted. "Tartan trousers!"

Hal shook his head and grinned at his uncle. "You got me."

The station ceremony was brief. Hal kept his eyes on the Atlas Diamond, but no one came within a yard of it, and Hadrian was there, constant as a shadow. When the royal couple stepped back onto the veranda, the whistle blew, and the crowd cheered as the Highland Falcon pulled away.

The train was swallowed by a tunnel as she traveled under Aberdeen. The glass of the observation car turned black, and the room was lit up by the carriage's electric chandeliers. The royal couple came inside, followed by a swirl of soot and smoke, and there was a smattering of applause from the guests.

Hal looked around the observation car at the chattering crowd. Amy was passing among them, offering drinks. It felt exactly like the night before, when Lydia Pickle's brooch disappeared.

Sierra put on a record, and music filled the carriage. "Here's to a wonderful last hurrah for the Highland Falcon and a delightful first hurrah for my darling friend and her handsome husband!" She lifted her glass, took a sip, and started dancing.

The princess laughed, and the prince held out his right hand. She took it, and he spun her into his left arm, a swift and impressive dance move. Hal watched as the Atlas Diamond swung away from her neck, its chain catching on the prince's lapel button. As the prince spun her back out, Hal watched aghast . . . as the necklace broke apart.

The egg-sized diamond dropped to the floor and shattered into a thousand pieces.

CHAPTER EIGHTEEN

A BROKEN ATLAS

Every person in the observation car gasped, but Sierra screamed. Then there was a long silence as they all stared at the smashed diamond, its fragments scattered across the floor.

Hal was no expert on diamonds, but he knew they shouldn't shatter. The princess looked like she was going to faint. Hal felt a firm hand on his shoulder. Uncle Nat was beside him as the train emerged from the tunnel and was flooded with light.

The prince hugged his wife to his side and cleared his throat. "Ladies and gentlemen, I'm afraid this evening's festivities must end abruptly." His expression was stony. "Hadrian, collect what is left of this necklace for the police."

The princess's eyes were full of tears.

"Don't be upset, darling. This is not the necklace I gave you." He lifted what was left of the chain from her neck, passing it to Hadrian. "This is a fake." He frowned. "The question is—where is the real one?"

Hal found himself being pushed toward the exit by his uncle. Somehow, Milo had done it! He looked back, scanning the room as if he were doing a superfast sketch, trying to absorb every detail he could see.

Had the necklace been switched for a fake, right in front of him, without him noticing? He looked ahead through the crowd in the corridor, searching for Milo, but there was no sign of the scowling man.

"I've said all along there was a thief on this train!" Mr. Pickle declared. "No one can deny it now."

"Let's go to our compartment," Uncle Nat said calmly.

Hal's heart jumped. He didn't know why, but he felt like he was in trouble.

***

125

Uncle Nat lowered the window blind and sat in his chair. Hal sat on the sofa.

"I need you to tell me the truth, Hal." Uncle Nat took off his glasses, wiping them on the corner of his jacket. "Mr. Pickle had mentioned that he saw you going into the royal carriage earlier this afternoon. Is that true?"

Hal nodded.

"You were staring at that necklace the whole time we were in Aberdeen." He put his glasses back on and blinked. "You even asked loudly if the princess was worried about it being stolen. It would be quite easy to think you knew it was going to happen."

"I didn't steal the necklace!"

"Of course you didn't." Uncle Nat leaned forward, looking directly into Hal's eyes. "But don't you think it's about time that you told me what you've been getting up to with Marlene Singh?"

"What?" Hal's mouth dropped open. "But . . . how did you know?"

Uncle Nat's laugh was soft. "I'm a journalist, Hal. It's my job to notice things. I saw Marlene peep at you through the window of the royal carriage in King's Cross. The last time I saw her, she was six. She loved trains even then. I knew you must have seen her, because you kept asking if there was another child on board." His eyebrows lifted. "When you stopped asking questions, I guessed you'd found her."

"I wanted to tell you," Hal said, relieved to be able to tell the truth, "but Lenny said her dad would get in trouble if anyone knew she was on board."

"That's why I haven't said anything." Uncle Nat leaned back.

"But she's not as discreet as she thinks she is." He chuckled. "And you've been on the trail of the jewel thief, have you?"

"The Magpie," Hal said, nodding. "We guessed the necklace was the target—well, Lenny did. I was meant to be keeping a watch out for any attempt to take it, but no one came anywhere near it." He shook his head. "I don't understand how it could have been stolen."

"The Magpie? Is that what you're calling the thief? Good name." Uncle Nat brought the tips of his fingers together. "Who's your prime suspect?"

"Milo Essenbach."

"The baron's son?"

"He's from a rich family, but he won't inherit any money because he's the youngest son . . . and he seems angry all the time," Hal explained. "He doesn't like trains, so why did he come on the Highland Falcon unless he's here for the jewels?"

"Do you have any proof?"

"Yes," Hal said. "We—" He stopped. "No . . . We have evidence, but no proof. We do know that Milo has an accomplice."

"An accomplice?" Uncle Nat blinked. "Tell you what, why don't I order dinner in the compartment tonight? I don't think anyone will want to eat in the dining car, and food is wonderfully helpful when puzzling through a mystery."

"Okay." Hal pulled out his sketchbook. "Do you mind if I do a quick sketch? I need to get down what I saw in the observation car when the diamond smashed, before my brain messes with the picture."

Hal dropped to the floor, wriggling onto his belly, and began to draw.

Uncle Nat buzzed the intercom to order dinner, then sat quietly as Hal drew.

When Amy arrived with the food, Hal closed his sketchbook, and the two of them sat on Uncle Nat's bunk to eat the flaky white cod in a buttery sauce. Hal told his uncle how he'd set out to catch a thief but instead had found Lenny. They'd both come to the conclusion the Magpie was Milo, but weren't sure who the accomplice was, although they suspected Sierra.

"I'm impressed." Uncle Nat dabbed sauce from his chin with a napkin. "And I didn't know about the secret lavatory in the library. *The Tudor Beard Tax*, you say? I must take a look."

"What do you think about Milo? He seems suspicious, right?"

"Yes—but the sparkling object he put in his pocket could have been something innocent. The note you found is a puzzle, but it doesn't explicitly mention stealing."

"What else could it mean?"

"I don't know." Uncle Nat shook his head.

"And what about when we found him acting strangely in the library?"

"He *was* rather jumpy," Uncle Nat admitted. "Doesn't make the man a thief, though."

"We were going to try to get proof before accusing him. We wanted to catch him in the act of stealing." Hal shrugged. "But the necklace has been stolen, so we've missed our chance." He sighed. "The police will probably solve it now."

"Can I see your drawings?"

Hal passed his book over. "They're just scribbles."

"These aren't scribbles, Hal. You've got a good eye." Uncle Nat looked impressed. "You've captured Lady Lansbury's hand gestures perfectly." He turned a page and snorted with laughter. "Steven Pickle, the sausage man! Ha! You've even got his flared nostrils."

Hal grinned. "He's a bit meaty."

"You're very observant." Uncle Nat tapped a finger to his lips. "The theft of the Atlas Diamond is a serious crime.

The police will be investigating it, but you have a head start. You may be able to help them. You may have seen something important, and with supervision from a responsible grown-up"—he pointed at himself—"I don't see why you shouldn't keep investigating. You never know, we might even solve the case first."

"Really?" Hal felt his body tingle with excitement.

"It can't hurt to try." Uncle Nat's eyes were sparkling. "You know, in all my adventures on trains, I've never had the opportunity to be a detective." He rubbed his hands together. "What should we do first?"

"I could draw the route of the Highland Falcon and plot the points where we think crimes happened," Hal said, "and places we've stopped for water and coal."

"Let's do it." Uncle Nat unpinned his map from the wall above his desk.

Sitting side by side on Uncle Nat's bed, the pair worked back through the journey, marking every moment of significance they could think of in Hal's book until, before they knew it, it was time for bed.

"You won't tell, will you?" Hal said, as he pulled his pajamas on. "About Lenny, I mean . . . being on the train."

"I've not seen any child on board this train but you." His uncle winked.

Hal lay in his bunk, certain he'd never sleep. He held his Saint Christopher between his thumb and forefinger as his mind whirled. He wished he could talk to Lenny about the necklace shattering. He wondered if she knew about it yet. He thought about her dad driving, and Joey shoveling coal into the furnace in the dark, and the Falcon's boiler huffing smoke and steam into the night. He pictured the train arcing in a grand curve across Scotland, sweeping into Banffshire, slipping through Elgin and the curved platform at Forres, rushing over the grand length of the Cullen viaduct . . .

And sleep arrived.

CHAPTER NINETEEN

A GRILLING FOR BREAKFAST

Hal slept fitfully, dreaming of robbers in stripy sweaters and black masks, as the Highland Falcon crossed the River Findhorn and skirted the edge of the Cairngorms National Park. He woke as the train halted in a siding at Dunblane. Sliding out of his bunk, he peeped round the blinds. A police officer was standing outside his window.

"What is it?" asked Uncle Nat, groggy with sleep.

"The police are outside," Hal whispered. "A whole line of them."

Uncle Nat got up, joining Hal at the window. "Interesting," he said. "They must think the thief is still on the train." Putting a finger to his lips, Uncle Nat left the blinds in place and silently slid the window down behind it.

The sound of rustling trees, dogs barking, and a pair of low voices came through the open window. Hal could see Rowan in pajamas and a bathrobe, supervising the dogs on their toilet break. Bailey sat quietly by his feet, looking sluggish, while Shannon and Fitzroy sniffed their way along the grass verge. Trafalgar and Viking barked excitedly at two officers walking alongside the carriages, each flanked by an obedient Alsatian.

"They've got sniffer dogs," Hal whispered.

"Bad news for the thief," said Uncle Nat, yawning. "Hello—what's this?" He bent down to pick up a piece of card that had been slid under their door. He waved the card. "We're summoned to the dining car at seven."

***

When Hal and his uncle entered the dining car, everyone was talking in hushed tones.

"A detective joined the train last night," Lucy Meadows said to Uncle Nat in a low voice. "Gordon's talking to her now—in the private dining room."

Steven Pickle folded his arms. "Finally, someone who'll do something about the thief." He glared at Hal.

Gordon Goulde came out of the private dining room, and the carriage fell silent. He was followed by a woman with cropped red hair, dressed in a gray polo shirt and a blue pantsuit. She stood in front of the guests and cleared her throat.

"Good morning, ladies and gentlemen. Sorry for the early start. I'm Detective Chief Inspector Bridget Clyde from the force in Inverness. His Royal Highness has asked me to investigate the theft of the Atlas Diamond." She took a gulp of coffee. "It's the prince's wish that we be discreet, which is why I'm talking to you in a siding at this ungodly hour. His Highness wishes that the press discover nothing of this incident until the Highland Falcon's tour is over."

133

She looked directly at Uncle Nat, who nodded.

"He doesn't want the scandal to, ah, *de-rail*"—she arched an eyebrow—"the planned festivities on the royal tour. Everything must continue as if nothing has happened. The prince and princess would be grateful for your support."

The guests murmured their approval.

"And hopefully, with your cooperation, we will find the criminal responsible for this ugly crime and return the necklace to the princess before we reach London." She surveyed the guests' faces. "This is a very serious crime. The Atlas Diamond is priceless, and we have good reason to suspect the thief is still among us. *Everyone* on the train is a suspect."

There were gasps.

"But how can you think that?" asked the baron, perplexed. "None of us have any idea when the necklace was taken."

"The princess was already wearing it when we met her at Balmoral!" Sierra insisted. "You should be talking to the castle staff."

"I will be interviewing each of you while my colleagues make a thorough search of the train," Inspector Clyde continued, ignoring the outcry. "None of you are to leave until I say so. But rest assured, we will find that necklace—and the thief." She took a moment to fix each of them with an icy stare. "Enjoy your breakfast." A smile twitched at the side of her mouth, and she returned to the private dining room.

The moment the door closed behind her, everyone in the dining car started talking.

"How ghastly," said Lady Lansbury. "What an ordeal for the poor princess."

"If I owned a diamond as big as the Atlas," Sierra said to Lucy, "no one would ever be able to steal it, because I'd never take it off. I'd even wear it in the shower."

***

Halfway through the breakfast service, the train pulled out of the siding and continued its journey south toward Glasgow.

"Excuse me, sir." Gordon Goulde stopped at their table to address Uncle Nat. "The Inspector would like to see you, followed by Master Beck."

"Thank you, Gordon. We'll go in together," Uncle Nat said, pulling his napkin from his collar and wiping his hands. "Come on, Hal." He dropped the napkin on the table and got to his feet.

In the private dining room, the brocade curtains were closed, so no one on the train could see in. Four armchairs were arranged around a table, one of which was occupied by Inspector Clyde. She signaled for Uncle Nat and Hal to sit down. A black-haired policeman with pimples slid the door shut behind them. "This is Detective Sergeant Prattle," said Inspector Clyde. "He'll be taking notes."

"I'm Nathaniel Bradshaw, and this is my nephew, Harrison Beck," Uncle Nat said, taking a seat. "I thought you might interview us together, seeing as I'm Hal's guardian."

Inspector Clyde nodded, and Sergeant Prattle took a record of their names.

"The first thing I need to know," said Inspector Clyde, "is whether either of you have visited the royal couple's compartment during your journey?"

"Is that where you suspect the necklace was taken from?" asked Uncle Nat.

"Yes," said Sergeant Prattle. "We think—"

"Sergeant Prattle," snapped Inspector Clyde. "Let him answer my question."

"No, I haven't visited the royal compartment," Uncle Nat replied.

Hal squirmed in his chair. If he told the truth, then he'd have to tell the detective about Lenny . . .

"And neither has Hal," Uncle Nat continued.

Hal shook his head, relieved that his uncle had answered for him.

"Have either of you seen or come into possession of a key to the royal compartment?"

"No," said Hal.

"I've not seen a key," said Uncle Nat. "Is one missing?"

Inspector Clyde didn't reply. "Please could you tell me your movements yesterday afternoon, from the moment you boarded the train at Ballater until the moment the necklace smashed."

"I ate a bit too much at Balmoral," admitted Uncle Nat. "I watched a little of the ceremony at Ballater but ducked out early, returning to my room for a nap. Hal can confirm that."

Hal nodded.

"And, Harrison, what were you doing while your uncle slept?"

"I went to the observation car to do some drawing." He put his sketchbook on the table and slid it toward the inspector. "You can take this as evidence, if you like."

"Evidence?" Inspector Clyde smiled.

"Yes. My pictures might help you solve the crime."

Sergeant Prattle snorted with laughter, and Inspector Clyde pushed the book back toward Hal. "I think you can keep it," she said. "We're not interested in children's pictures."

Hal felt his face go red. He took the book off the table and hugged it to his chest.

"How long did you stay in the observation car?"

"I drew for about half an hour. Isaac was on the veranda taking pictures, and Milo Essenbach was there for a little bit, but he complained about the cold and left. Then, I had scones in the gentlemen's lounge. Lady Lansbury was in there with Rowan . . ." Hal paused. "I couldn't eat one of the scones because of the big lunch, and I'd heard the train crew say it was Graham the train guard's birthday. So I decided to give him a scone as a birthday cake. I took it to the service cars, but I couldn't find him." He shrugged. "So I left it."

"So, you *have* been into the royal carriage?" Inspector Clyde stared at him. Her eyes were steely blue.

"I went *through* the carriage but not into the compartment," Hal replied. "The security man said I could go through, and Hadrian—the guard—was standing outside the door."

"I see," said Inspector Clyde, making a note. "Did you see or hear anything out of the ordinary?"

Hal shook his head.

"And what did you do after that?"

"I went to the observation car to see the celebrations as we came into Aberdeen, and then the necklace smashed."

"This case is quite a puzzler," Uncle Nat said. "I presume you're asking us about our movements between Ballater and

Aberdeen because that's when you think the necklace was taken and switched for the fake?"

"The only thing we know for certain is that the necklace the princess took out of the safe and put on yesterday morning in Balmoral was the real one," Inspector Clyde replied.

"She's taken it off only once," Sergeant Prattle added.

"Really?" Uncle Nat leaned forward.

Sergeant Prattle nodded. "At all other times, the diamond has been in the view of five or more people."

Inspector Clyde cleared her throat, looking sternly at Sergeant Prattle. "What Sergeant Prattle means to say is that the interview is over for now. We're grateful for your cooperation."

"Glad to be of service," Uncle Nat said politely. "Although you really shouldn't dismiss my nephew's sketches so quickly."

"Mr. Bradshaw"—Inspector Clyde sighed—"I'm not a babysitter."

Hal stared at the wall above the inspector's head, trying not to get angry. He'd only been trying to help.

"I've got a job to do," Inspector Clyde continued, pointing a finger at Uncle Nat. "And if a whisper about this theft makes its way into any newspaper, I'll be coming to you for an explanation. I'm not a fan of journalists."

"Understood." Uncle Nat bowed his head.

"Good," she said. "In that case, you're free to go." She paused. "For now."

"Thank you, Detective Chief Inspector," Uncle Nat said, rising from his seat. "Come along, Hal."

But Hal didn't hear him. There was a brass air vent above the inspector's head, and something behind it was moving.

"Hal?"

Hal jumped. "Sorry. Coming."

Inspector Clyde shook her head. "Sergeant Prattle, please show the next guest in."

***

"Well, she's formidable," Uncle Nat said as they returned to their table in the dining car.

"She's mean," Hal said quietly, "and rude."

Uncle Nat nodded. "That, too," he said, pouring himself a cup of tea. "But"—he leaned across the table and lowered his voice to a whisper—"we did at least learn for certain when the police think the diamond was stolen."

"We did?" Hal's eyes grew wide as he realized that Uncle Nat had been using the interview to get information.

"We did. The real necklace was removed from the safe in Balmoral yesterday morning and placed around the neck of the princess. According to Sergeant Prattle, she has taken it off only once, and that must have been when we were traveling from Ballater to Aberdeen, else they wouldn't be asking about it. Whoever swapped the necklace for the fake must have seized the opportunity to make the switch while she was getting dressed in the royal compartment." He sat back and grinned at Hal. "To be honest, I understand why police officers dislike journalists. We're a wily bunch." He waggled his eyebrows.

"Uncle Nat, you know that secret thing that we talked about last night?"

"Yes."

"I need to . . . um . . ." He didn't want to mention Lenny in the dining car in case anyone heard.

"Pop off somewhere?"

Hal nodded. "I'm not sure how long the thing can be secret for, if you know what I mean."

"I do. Yes." He drained his teacup. "I shall go back to the compartment. I have a lot of writing to do. This mystery is a gift to a novelist. If it becomes a book, I might want to use some of your drawings."

"Really?"

"I'd pay you for them, of course." Uncle Nat got up. "Right. Good luck, and keep your eyes peeled for clues."

***

Hal walked past the private dining room, as if he were heading to the library. When he reached the sliding door, he turned, eyeing up a cupboard built into the corner. He opened the door a crack and peered inside. He saw crockery, an empty champagne bucket stuffed with cutlery, and—perched on the highest shelf on a neatly folded pile of tablecloths—he saw Lenny.

"Quick!" she hissed. "Get in!"

Hal climbed up beside her. Lenny pulled the cupboard door shut, plunging them into darkness.

"What are you doing?" Hal whispered, trying to get comfortable.

"I came in here to get away from the dogs," Lenny whispered in his ear. "They're all over the staff carriages. I didn't realize they'd do the police interviews next door."

"You shouldn't be here," Hal whispered. "You'll get caught."

"Listen"—Lenny pointed to the grate—"I'm learning loads."

CHAPTER TWENTY

SPIES AND ALIBIS

Hal pulled out his sketchbook and pen as he peered through the grate. He could see the back of Inspector Clyde's head. Isaac was lounging in the armchair, nodding.

"Isaac Adebayo, it says here that you are the royal photographer."

"I am."

"Do you have keys to any of the rooms in the royal carriage?"

Isaac laughed. "Nobody ever gives their keys to a photographer."

"Could you tell us your movements yesterday afternoon, from when you boarded the train at Ballater, until the reception in Aberdeen?"

Isaac explained that he'd taken photographs of the royal couple boarding the train at Ballater, and then moved to set up in the observation car.

"I followed the royal couple out onto the veranda to photograph them with the Lord Mayor, and then saw the necklace smash along with everyone else—but we were in a tunnel. I didn't get the picture." He shook his head.

"Can anyone confirm your account?"

"Anyone and everyone," Isaac replied. "Hal was in the observation car, and Milo Essenbach was there."

"Harrison Beck?" said Inspector Clyde. The hairs on Hal's neck stood up. "Mr. Pickle claims he is the thief. He said the boy was, and I quote, 'following the princess about like a lost dog and couldn't take his eyes off the diamond.'"

"Mr. Pickle doesn't like children. Harrison Beck is a good kid." Isaac shook his head. "Who can blame him for mooning around after the princess and having a little crush?"

Hal's jaw dropped open, and Lenny clamped her hands over her mouth to keep from laughing.

Isaac was dismissed and replaced by Sierra Knight, who perched swanlike on her seat.

Inspector Clyde addressed Sierra from her seat across the table. "Ms. Knight, do you hold any keys to the royal compartment?"

"Oh goodness, no!" Sierra let out a trill of laughter. "I don't even keep the key to my own room. Lucy looks after it. She's my assistant, although we're more like best friends, really."

"Could you tell us what you were doing yesterday afternoon from the moment you stepped onto the train, until after the reception in Aberdeen?"

"Lucy and I were in our compartment, running through my lines for *Thoroughly Modern Millie*. It's my next West End show and . . ."

"You were together in your compartment all afternoon?"

"Yes, until we reached Aberdeen." Sierra smiled. "Lucy will tell you exactly the same thing."

"She's lying," Hal whispered in Lenny's ear. "I saw Lucy in the library, reading a book."

"There was a small, sensitive matter that I wanted to mention." Sierra cleared her throat. "Um, you see . . ."

"We're aware of your criminal record, Ms. Knight."

"Oh, you are?" Sierra blushed. "I was very young. I—"

"Theft is theft, Ms. Knight. But shoplifting lipstick is hardly the same as stealing a priceless diamond."

"No! Of course not."

"Right. I think that concludes my questions for now," Inspector Clyde said.

"Yes—thank you." Sierra got up and began backing out of the room, pausing by the door. "Oh, there is something else I felt I should mention. The boy, Harrison—just before we got to Aberdeen, he said the strangest thing. He asked the princess if she was worried about her necklace getting stolen. We laughed at the time, but now it seems a bit odd, doesn't it?"

Lenny turned to Hal. "You idiot," she hissed. "What did you say that for?"

"I don't know. It just came out."

***

Lucy Meadows was the next guest to be interviewed.

"Ms. Knight tells us you look after the keys to her room," said Inspector Clyde. "Is that correct?"

Lucy nodded. "I look after *everything* for her. I manage her appointment book, answer her phone, and pack her luggage." She sighed. "It's my job."

"Ms. Knight also says you're good friends . . ."

"I don't get my friends to pick up my dirty underwear—do you?"

"Ha!" Inspector Clyde laughed. "No, I do not. Do you have keys to any other part of the train, Miss Meadows?"

"No." Lucy replied.

"Sierra Knight and the princess are friends, are they not?"

"They are, but they're not as close as Sierra makes out," Lucy said. "I've not set foot in the royal carriage since boarding the train, and neither has Sierra."

"You're certain?"

Lucy nodded. "There's very little I don't know about Sierra Knight."

"Ms. Knight tells us you were running through lines for a play in her compartment yesterday afternoon?"

"Yes. I could probably recite the whole play for you, if you liked."

"No, you're all right." Inspector Clyde chuckled.

"Lucy's lying, too!" Hal whispered. "Why? What are they hiding?"

"Lucy's not lying to protect Sierra, that's for sure," Lenny replied. "She doesn't even like her."

"Then why didn't she tell the truth?"

"You didn't tell the truth," Lenny said, grinning. "Perhaps she's protecting someone else."

"You heard that, then?"

"Yes." She gave him a gentle pinch. "Thanks for not snitching on me."

***

Ten minutes later, Lady Lansbury entered the interview room with Trafalgar, who sat by her chair. Inspector Clyde was deferential, but she asked Lady Lansbury the same questions she'd asked everyone else.

Lady Lansbury replied that she didn't have keys to the royal compartment and had spent the afternoon in the gentlemen's lounge—first alone, and then with her gentleman-in-waiting, speaking about her darling dogs.

Hal nodded. "I saw her."

Baron Essenbach was next to be brought in, followed by Ernest White. Each confirmed that they had been playing billiards in the game room with the other.

"Do you think Ernest could be Milo's accomplice?" Lenny whispered.

"What makes you say that?"

"He used to do Gordon's job. He could still have his old keys from when he used to be the head steward."

Hal frowned. "But he loves the royal family."

"Well, Milo's getting help from *someone*." Lenny shrugged. "It would make sense if it was someone who knows this train like the back of their hand."

"I suppose he could do with the money," Hal replied. "And he thought it was funny when Lydia Pickle lost her brooch."

Next, Sergeant Prattle showed in Rowan Buck. Inspector Clyde quizzed him about his movements, and Rowan explained that he hadn't attended the Aberdeen reception with the other guests and did not have an alibi for the journey from Ballater because he'd been tending the dogs, only leaving them briefly to speak with Lady Lansbury.

"No alibi," Lenny whispered.

Hal shook his head. "But I saw him with Lady Lansbury, and

then later on with the dogs in their cabin when I brought you the scones. He's telling the truth."

Milo Essenbach was next to stroll into the room, and Hal grabbed Lenny's arm. The two pushed their faces against the grate.

"Mr. Essenbach," Inspector Clyde said, "have you seen or had access to a key to the royal compartment?"

"Nope," said Milo. "I have not."

"What were your movements yesterday afternoon after you boarded the train?"

"I went to the observation car to read the paper, but it was freezing. The photographer kept opening the doors to the veranda, so I went to my room and stayed there," Milo replied.

"All afternoon?"

"I came out for the flag waving in Aberdeen." He smiled his crooked smile. "My father asked me to. I left as soon as that silly bauble smashed."

"You think a priceless diamond is a silly bauble?"

"It's pretty." Milo shrugged. "But what good does it do anyone?"

"He doesn't have an alibi," hissed Lenny as Milo Essenbach got up to leave his interview. "And Sierra is lying about hers."

Hal peeped back through the grate just as Gordon walked in.

Inspector Clyde stood up. "Mr. Goulde, thank you for letting us use the private dining room for our interviews." She gestured to a chair. "Sit down, will you?"

Gordon Goulde took the seat opposite, wringing his hands.

"You hold a set of keys for all the doors on this train, including the royal compartment, is that correct?"

"Yes, that's right."

"Is there anyone else on the train who might have a key for the royal compartment?"

"There are three keys," said Gordon. "The other two are in the possession of the royal couple and their security guard, Hadrian. When they aren't traveling on the train, the keys are kept in the bedside drawer of the royal bedroom. They were collected by security when the royal couple boarded the train."

"Does that mean anyone could have walked into the compartment on the way up from London and taken one of the keys to make a copy?" asked Inspector Clyde.

"It was locked until they arrived," Gordon explained. "I let them in using my key."

"Do other members of staff have keys?"

"No," said Gordon. "Only me."

"And do you ever leave your keys unattended?"

Gordon stiffened. "No, I do not."

"Very well—I think that concludes our interviews for the moment. Sergeant Prattle and I will check the progress of the search and speak to the rest of your staff this afternoon."

Inspector Clyde and Sergeant Prattle stood up and followed Gordon Goulde out, leaving the room empty.

Lenny turned to Hal. "He does leave his keys unattended."

"You think Milo stole the key to the compartment?"

"No—*I* did. That's how I got into the compartment in King's Cross. I put it back, though, once I'd got one of the keys from the drawer inside."

"Lenny!"

"What?" She frowned. "Don't look at me like that."

"What did you do with that key?"

"I put it back when we were at Ballater, before the security sweep," Lenny explained.

"You left the door unlocked?"

"No, I locked it—and then slipped the key underneath the door."

"Then the Magpie must have gotten into the royal compartment after you left it but before the prince and princess got on the train."

Lenny nodded. "And the Magpie would know how to pick the lock. They wouldn't need a key. I'm surprised Inspector Clyde hasn't thought of that."

"I'm sure she has," Hal said. "Well, Milo and Sierra are the only people who don't have an alibi for the time the necklaces were switched. She's got to be his accomplice."

"There is one other person," said Lenny.

"Who?"

"Your uncle."

CHAPTER TWENTY-ONE

BATTY MOSS

Hal shifted uncomfortably. His right leg was dead, and his stomach had gulped with alarm at the possibility his uncle might be the Magpie. He pushed the thought to the back of his mind. He was sure Uncle Nat wasn't a thief.

"You can't stay in here," he said to Lenny. "Why don't you hide in our compartment?"

"But your uncle . . ."

"He knows about you."

"*What?* You promised you wouldn't tell anyone."

"I didn't. He figured it out. He's pretty clever, you know. Anyway, he's on our side."

"He is?"

"Yes. Now help me figure out how to get you into our room without someone seeing you." He thought for a moment. "I could bring Uncle Nat's hat and raincoat to disguise you. We're only a few doors past the dining car. There are loads of police walking up and down the train—perhaps no one will notice."

"That's
a terrible idea."
Lenny made a face. "No
one would believe I'm a man."

"Do you have a better plan?"

Lenny shook her head.

"Right, then. Stay here—I'll go and get you a disguise."

Hal slipped out of the cupboard and returned to the compartment.

"You missed the sniffer dogs," Uncle Nat said as he came in. "The police have gone through the rooms." He was folding his clothes. "It's official: we're not harboring stolen jewelry."

Hal felt reassured. He knew his uncle was not a thief.

Uncle Nat looked out the window, pushing his glasses up his nose. "Oh, look, Hal—the Yorkshire Dales." He stood up. "This is where your nana and papa were from." He sighed, gazing out at the craggy windswept hills. "To me, the Settle to Carlisle Railway line is the most beautiful in the world." He looked back at Hal. "When my time comes, I think I'd like my ashes scattered here."

"Like
Lady Lansbury's
husband?" Hal approached the
window as the train rattled onto a viaduct,
which soared over a valley. A silver river glimmered
below.

"Why not? This is the Batty Moss Viaduct. Isn't that a wonderful name?"

Overwhelmed with vertigo-infused wonder, Hal looked at his grinning uncle and caught a glimpse of the boy he once was. He took a deep breath. "Uncle Nat, I need your help. Lenny is trapped in a cupboard in the dining car."

"She's what?" Uncle Nat blinked.

"She hid there, not knowing the police would use the private dining room for their interviews, and now she can't get out. Can she hide in here? Just till things calm down."

"I'm not sure things *will* calm down," Uncle Nat said. "It might be a good time for Lenny to come clean and tell the police she's on board. I'm sure they'd understand. They might already know."

"But . . . I promised. *You* promised."

"Fine. Bring her here, and when we next stop for coal and water, I'll go and have a word with Mohanjit. He must know she can't hide for much longer."

"Can I borrow your hat and coat?"

"What on earth for?"

"For a disguise."

"What are you disguising her as, a pint-sized gangster?" Uncle Nat chuckled. "That'll never work."

"She can't just walk here as herself. She's a stowaway. If anyone sees her, she'll be in trouble."

"Hmm . . . often the best place to hide something is in full view." Uncle Nat tapped a finger to his lip. "You said she was in a cupboard?"

"Yes, full of tablecloths and napkins—stuff for the dining car."

"Great—then that's what you'll use."

"Dress her as a ghost?"

"Ha! It's not Halloween yet, Hal. No—but I do have an idea."

***

Hal returned to the cupboard, checking the coast was clear before quietly knocking.

"Quick—get out!" he hissed, and Lenny jumped down. "Hold your arms out in front of you," he instructed, taking a pile of tablecloths and stacking them high on her outstretched forearms. "If anyone comes toward you, lift the tablecloths so they can't see your face."

"What if someone comes up behind me?" Lenny asked.

"I'll be standing behind you holding this newspaper up as if I'm reading it. Walk quickly and confidently, but don't run. Go, go, go!"

Lenny hurried forward, keeping her face hidden behind the pile of white linen, and Hal followed. The dining car was empty. They passed the kitchen, making it into the corridor of the sleeping car, when Lenny stopped abruptly.

"Someone's coming!" she hissed. "It's the Pickles!"

"Don't panic," Hal said, feeling like ice-cold frogs were hopping about inside his tummy. "Keep going."

"I won't be able to get past them!" Lenny squeaked, pushing her face against the tablecloths. "They're going to see me."

Hal peeped round her. The Pickles were two steps away from his compartment.

The door sprang open.

"Ah, Mr. Pickle!" Uncle Nat stepped into the hallway in front of Lenny. "Just the man I wanted to see."

"Hiya!" Lydia Pickle smiled.

"The police have been through our things with two sniffer dogs, and you'll be glad to hear they found nothing. No necklaces, no earrings, no brooches." Uncle Nat stepped sideways and discreetly gestured to Hal.

Hal took the cue from his uncle and quickly shoved Lenny into the compartment, motioning for her to hide behind the door.

Uncle Hal frowned. "Aren't you going to apologize for accusing my nephew of being a thief?"

"I most certainly am not!" Mr. Pickle huffed. "Now, get out of my way."

Uncle Nat and Hal stepped back into the cabin doorway and watched the Pickles exit the corridor.

"That was close!" Hal said, closing the door behind them.

"Thank you, Mr. Bradshaw," Lenny said. "You saved my bacon."

"My pleasure, Marlene. You probably don't remember me, but we met when you were little."

"I do." Lenny grinned. "Dad's got all your books; he reads them to me. They're brilliant."

"Aren't you kind." Uncle Nat beamed. "Now, we'll be pulling into Settle soon, to take on coal and water. So, I'm going to talk to your father. I think he should tell the police you're on the train, Marlene. I'm sure everyone will understand why you wanted to come on this journey." He looked at Hal. "Lock the door and don't open it to anyone except me. If the police discover a stowaway, it'll take some explaining." He picked up his journal and pen. "I won't be long."

Lenny threw herself on the sofa as Hal locked the door behind his uncle. "We don't have much time," she said.

"For what?"

"To solve the mystery of the Highland Falcon Thief!" Lenny rested her chin on her hands. "Once people find out I'm here, they'll probably send me home. If Milo is the thief and Sierra his accomplice, we'll have to get proof quick."

"How?"

"I'm glad you asked." Lenny waggled her eyebrows. "Because I've got a plan."

CHAPTER TWENTY-TWO

UNSETTLED
AT SETTLE

"I've been to Settle station before," Lenny said. "The loco has to pull the front of the train beyond the platform to take on coal and water. All the formal duties, the handshaking with the prince and princess, will happen at the back, on the veranda of the observation car. Everyone will be down at that end of the train."

"So?" Hal sat on Uncle Nat's chair.

"So, that's when we search Milo's compartment."

"But the police have already searched it and found no jewels."

"We're not looking for jewels. We're looking for proof that he's the Magpie. We might find tools or plans."

"But the door will be locked." Hal looked at Lenny's tool belt. "Can you pick locks?"

"I wish! I wouldn't have borrowed Gordon's key to the royal compartment if I could pick locks."

"But I promised Uncle Nat I wouldn't leave."

"No, you didn't." Lenny crossed her arms. "You promised him you'd lock the door when he left and not open it to anyone but him. And I'm not suggesting we go out the door. I'm saying we should go out the window."

"*What?*"

"It'll be easy. When we pull into Settle, the window will be on the opposite side to the platform. No one will see us. We'll open it and climb out. I'll jimmy Milo's window open with my screwdriver." She pointed to her tool belt. "We'll get in and scout the place as fast as we can, making sure we get back before the train pulls out of the station." She waited for a response. "C'mon, Hal—otherwise Inspector Clyde will catch Milo and get the reward, and we worked it out *first*."

Hal nodded. "I suppose."

"Good." Lenny jumped up. "Which one is Milo's—do you know?"

"He's next door. That way." Hal pointed at the opposite wall.

"Easy-peasy."

"It's a big drop to the ground," said Hal.

"So don't let go." Lenny pushed her face against the glass. "Come on—the train's slowing down already."

The train pulled through the idyllic Settle station. Hal saw a white-and-cherry-red building with a slate roof and frilly wooden trim, but his pulse was racing. As soon as they'd passed the platform and drawn to a halt, Lenny jumped on the chair and opened the window. She climbed out sideways, swinging her left leg out.

"Let's go," she hissed, one foot on the thin metal ledge

beneath the window. She reached out, full stretch, hooking the fingers of her left hand around the window of Milo's room, before swinging her leg across, so that she was straddling the two windows.

"Be careful!" Hal whispered.

Lenny pulled the screwdriver from her tool belt and prized Milo's window open. Hal's heart was beating so fast, he thought he might throw up. Once Lenny had pushed the window down, she got her hand inside and brought her right leg and arm over and clambered in, before sticking her head back out and grinning at Hal.

"Come on," she said. "Now you."

Hal stood on the chair and stepped one leg out the window, reaching unsuccessfully for the edge of Milo's window.

"Try reaching with your foot first," Lenny hissed.

Hal gripped the window frame and stretched out his leg as far as he could; the chair wobbled and he gasped. His hands were sweating. He froze, feeling that at any moment, he might fall onto the tracks. "I can't do it," he said. "I'll fall."

"You won't. It's only a few feet, anyway."

Hal gripped the window tighter. His arms were shaking. "It's too high." He heard the panic in his own voice. "I can't do it."

"You can. Here—grab my hand."

Hal looked across. Her hand seemed miles away. He shook his head.

"Okay—don't worry," said Lenny, smiling reassuringly. "Go back inside, and I'll tell you what I see."

Hal pulled himself back into the compartment, tumbling onto the floor with relief and shame. He grabbed his sketchbook and put his head back out of the window so he could hear Lenny.

"It's the mirror image of yours," he heard her say. "Except Milo is very messy."

Hal whipped lines onto the page, creating the reverse image of his cabin. "Tell me everything you can see."

"There's paper everywhere," said Lenny. "All over the desk. Screwed up in balls all over the carpet . . ." She fell silent. "I've opened a couple—they all have one word or a few sentences, but always scribbled out. It's like he's trying to write an important letter but can't think of the right words."

"What else?"

"Ugh . . . stinky socks. A stack of books on the floor—poetry by John Donne and e. e. cummings. He hasn't unpacked—there's a duffel bag in front of the wardrobe. His clothes are spilling out. I'm looking inside . . ." There was a silence. "Nope—just clothes."

"Start in one corner of the room and tell me everything you see," Hal said, his pen finishing off the outline of a duffel bag.

"Okay. Above the sofa, dangling from a lamp, is a blue-and-pink-spotted silk scarf. Milo's coat is hanging off the back of the door . . ." There was another moment of silence, followed by a gasp. "The note's gone from the pocket! . . . Oh, Hal!" Her head popped out of the window. "There's a bracelet in the soap well by the sink. It looks like diamonds!"

"Don't touch it," Hal said. "Describe it to me."

"It's a circlet of gold, and embedded in it, one after another, are small diamonds. Why didn't the police find this when they searched?"

"The men with dogs weren't looking for a bracelet," said Hal. "They probably thought it was Milo's—" The Highland Falcon let out a high whistle, making Hal jump. "Lenny, get out of there. We're about to move."

"Hang on! I forgot to check the drawer under the seat."

"Lenny, come on."

"There's a suitcase in here."

"Leave it . . . Lenny?" Hal held his breath, puffing it out when her grinning head stuck out of Milo's window. "Don't do that to me."

The smile fell from her lips, and her head turned. "Someone's trying to get in! I've got to hide!" She disappeared from view.

"Lenny?" Hal whispered. "*Lenny!*"

There was no reply.

A whoosh of steam, and the Highland Falcon lurched forward, pulling away from the station.

CHAPTER TWENTY-THREE

STEAM OF THE DRAGON

Hal opened the wardrobe door, pushing his head against the wall they shared with Milo, expecting to hear Lenny cry out or Milo's angry shout. He listened but heard nothing. Grabbing a glass from beside the sink, he held it against the wall, putting his ear to it. There was a thump and a clattering sound. Hal jumped back. "Lenny!" He tossed the glass onto the sofa, flipped the key, and yanked open the door.

"Whoa!" Uncle Nat was standing in the hall, his hand raised to knock.

"Hi." Hal stuck his head into the hall, glancing up and down. It was empty. Milo's door was closed.

"I spoke to your father . . . Oh." Uncle Nat looked about. "Where's Lenny?"

"Um . . ." Hal blinked. He didn't want to tell Uncle Nat that she'd broken into Milo's compartment. "She's in the bathroom."

"Oh. I'll wait till she gets back." Uncle Nat sat down on the sofa. "I thought she was worried about being seen."

"She was desperate. She thought she could risk it because everyone was at the other end of the train for the Settle celebration, but now I'm worried she might be stuck in the toilet. I'll go and check."

Hal stepped out into the corridor and shut the door behind him, waited for a second to be sure Uncle Nat wasn't going to open it again, and then crept to Milo's compartment.

The door was closed. There was no sound from within. If Milo had found Lenny, there would have been a row, which meant she must be hidden, trapped in there with Milo.

"What are you doing, boy?"

Hal jumped. Mr. Pickle was striding toward him.

"Loitering? Plotting to steal something?"

"I'm . . . going to the library to get a book," Hal said defiantly, marching past the horrible man.

"Are you, now?" Mr. Pickle turned and followed Hal. "Why don't I believe you?"

As Hal walked, he tried not to panic. Lenny was stuck in Milo's compartment, and he was being driven the wrong way up the train by a suspicious Steven Pickle. He wished he'd told Uncle Nat the truth. As he passed through the dining car, he racked his brains for a reason to turn around, but he didn't want Mr. Pickle accompanying him back to Milo's room. Arriving in the library, he went straight to the nearest shelf and pulled out a book.

Mr. Pickle entered a moment later, scowling at Hal as he stomped past. "I've got my eye on you, boy," he said. "Every move you make, I'm watching." He lingered, making sure Hal felt the full force of his menacing glare.

The other library door slid open behind him.

"Oh!" Lucy Meadows exclaimed, surprised to see Mr. Pickle's back.

"Beg your pardon, Miss Meadows," Mr. Pickle said, moving past her as he left the library.

Lucy made a beeline for a low bookshelf, grabbing a book and opening it.

Hal stepped backward toward the near door, worried Mr. Pickle would return, but desperate to get back and help Lenny.

Lucy gasped. "Oh! Hal!" she said, snapping her book shut. "I didn't see you there."

"Sorry. Didn't mean to make you jump." Hal smiled politely, pointing at the book she was holding. "Is it good?"

"Excuse me?"

"That book," Hal said. "*Steam of the Dragon*."

"Oh! Yes—I love dragons."

Hal frowned. "Don't you mean *trains*?"

"Of course! Trains and dragons." Lucy nodded vigorously. "Anyway, I must go—Sierra's waiting." She tucked the book under her arm, and as she marched past Hal, something slipped from between its pages, falling to the floor.

"Wait!" Hal called after her, crouching down to pick up the plain blue envelope. But when he looked back up, Lucy had already disappeared.

Hal turned the envelope over in his hands. The flap was tucked in, not sealed. He felt a ripple of guilt as he opened it and slid out a rectangle of folded paper. Written in a sharp, spidery hand, he read:

My darling,

I am miserable. Seeing you every day and pretending we barely know each other is torture. I want to tell the world I love you, but instead I'm leaving notes in books like a desperate schoolboy.

Look what you've done to me. I understand you feel it has to be this way, that we should hide our love from the world's prying for a little longer, but I want you to know you are in every one of my waking thoughts.

M.

Hearing the *clip-clop* of high heels, Hal pushed the note back into the envelope and stuffed it in his pocket.

"Have you seen Lucy anywhere?" Sierra asked as she pushed the other library door open. Her eyes darted about the room. She was obviously annoyed.

"She came through a minute ago." Hal pointed at the near door.

Sierra tutted. "She was meant to be getting something for me."

"If I see her, I'll tell her you're looking for her," Hal said, smiling awkwardly as Sierra strutted past him.

As the door closed on Sierra, Hal clapped his hands over his face. They'd gotten *everything* wrong. Milo was in love with Sierra Knight! Lucy had been carrying their love notes. That's why Sierra had made Lucy lie for her. Her alibi was that she was with Milo. He wasn't the Magpie at all! Hal pulled out his sketchbook, flicking to the page with Milo's note, and he reread it, realizing his mistake. The bracelet Lenny had seen in his compartment probably belonged to Sierra—and the pink-and-blue polka-dot scarf likely did, too. He had to get back to Lenny and tell her.

The door behind him to the billiards room opened again. He held his breath expecting Mr. Pickle's voice.

"Hello, Harrison." It was Milo. "Reading more of your uncle's books?"

Hal's heart skipped a beat. How could Milo be coming from that end of the train? He was supposed to be in his compartment, with Lenny. If he *wasn't* in there, then who was?

"Are you all right?" Milo asked. "You've gone very pale."

But Hal didn't reply. He was already racing out of the library.

CHAPTER TWENTY-FOUR

THE TURN OF THE KEY

Hal sprinted through the dining car, bumping into Sergeant Prattle, who blocked his path with an outstretched hand.

"Stop," said the sergeant.

"I'm in a rush," Hal said, as the loudspeaker crackled, and Gordon Goulde's voice boomed through the train.

"Ladies and gentlemen, Detective Chief Inspector Clyde has asked that all guests gather in the dining car as a matter of urgency. Please make your way there *immediately*."

"Not anymore, you're not." Sergeant Prattle pointed to a seat. "Sit down."

The carriage began filling with guests.

"I hope this means the necklace has been found," the baron said, sitting at the table next to Hal's. "We can enjoy the rest of the journey in peace."

"There's never a dull moment on the Highland Falcon," said Milo, sitting opposite his father, wearing a sardonic smile.

Uncle Nat spotted Hal and joined him.

"Did you leave our compartment door unlocked?" Hal whispered. "For Lenny."

"Of course," his uncle replied.

Hal bit his lip. If everyone came to the dining car, hopefully that would give Lenny a chance to slip out of Milo's room.

Lady Lansbury arrived, followed by Rowan. He stood by the door with Bailey, Shannon, and Trafalgar.

Shannon and Trafalgar yapped and jumped up as Sierra entered the carriage.

"Get them off me!" she squealed, leaning away. "Urgh, dogs!" She went and sat at the other end of the carriage.

Hal thought he saw Lucy smile, but he was more concerned that Bailey seemed downcast and lethargic. She wasn't jumping around with the other dogs.

"Now, now, girls," soothed Lady Lansbury. "Be on your best behavior for the nice detectives."

"This is the least relaxing train journey I've ever been on," grumbled Steven Pickle, dropping into a chair. "You wouldn't get this on one of *my* trains."

"You wouldn't get a *seat* on one of your trains," muttered Ernest White from behind him.

The prince and princess were the last to enter, and both wore grave expressions. As they sat, Inspector Clyde arose from the corner, and everyone turned to face her.

"Thank you for coming," she said. "I apologize for the disruption, but I wanted to inform you that, although we have not yet located the princess's necklace, we *have* taken a suspect into custody." A smile flickered across her face as an intrigued murmur rippled through the carriage.

"Who is it?" asked Lydia Pickle. "Did you find my brooch?"

"The thief has been walking among you since the Highland Falcon left London," Inspector Clyde said. "The necklace was taken . . . by a stowaway."

"Oh no," Uncle Nat said under his breath as everyone gasped. Hal felt sick.

"A stowaway! On the royal train!" exclaimed Lady Lansbury. "How is that possible?"

"Her name is Marlene Singh," said Inspector Clyde. "She is the daughter of the royal train driver, Mohanjit Singh, who at this minute is driving the Highland Falcon toward . . . um . . ."

"Blackburn," said Uncle Nat quietly.

"He is the mastermind behind the thefts. Devastated that the Highland Falcon is being retired, angry at losing his job, and with children to feed, Mohanjit has resorted to stealing. He smuggled his daughter onto the train to lift valuable jewelry from the Highland Falcon's wealthy guests."

Hal leaped up. "That's not true!"

"Friends of yours, are they?" Steven Pickle sneered. "Should have known."

Uncle Nat tried to get Hal to sit down.

"Where's your proof?" Hal shouted, his fists clenched.

"Right here," said Sergeant Prattle, lifting a brown envelope and removing a small stuffed toy with a pair of plastic tweezers. It was Penny Mouse.

"This toy was found inside the wardrobe of the royal bedroom," said Inspector Clyde. "Mr. Singh has confirmed this mouse belongs to his daughter. Mr. Singh took Gordon Goulde's key to the royal compartment and gave it to Marlene, who concealed herself in the royal wardrobe at Ballater. When the princess boarded the train, the girl waited until she was getting changed and switched the diamond pendant for the glass fake."

A phone went off. Everyone turned to look at Steven Pickle, but it was Inspector Clyde who answered her mobile.

"Hello?" she said. "Speaking. As we thought. Thanks." She hung up. "That was confirmation that Marlene Singh's fingerprints were found on a key to the royal compartment discovered on the floor by the door."

Hal sat down with a bump.

"What about my brooch?" Lydia Pickle asked.

"We believe the train driver and his daughter have used their intimate knowledge of the train to hide the jewels," Inspector Clyde explained. "Our dogs have been unable to find anything. But once the train has returned to London, we will find your jewelry."

Hal stood up. "Lenny would *never* steal anything," he said, shaking his head.

"Then I'm sure you can explain why we found the lock to Milo Essenbach's compartment broken and Marlene Singh inside," Inspector Clyde said triumphantly.

"My room?" Milo was surprised.

"We searched the suspect and found nothing, but should you notice anything missing when you return to your compartment, please report it to me. I'm afraid she made quite a mess in there."

"But, she didn't—" Hal began, but Uncle Nat spoke over him.

"What about the tour of the Highland Falcon?" he asked in a clear voice. "If the train driver is—"

"The prince would like the tour to continue as planned,"

Inspector Clyde interrupted, and the prince nodded. "Marlene Singh is being held in the luggage car until we reach London. Regrettably, we are unable to replace her father, as there are few people qualified to drive the Highland Falcon. He will continue to drive the train under police guard until we reach Paddington, where he will be formally charged and placed under arrest."

Hal opened his mouth to protest, but Uncle Nat gripped him by the shoulder, making him sit down again, and shook his head in warning.

"We ask that you keep this information to yourselves until the Highland Falcon arrives in London, at which point Scotland Yard will take control of the investigation."

CHAPTER TWENTY-FIVE

STATIONERY OBSERVATIONS

"The police are wrong! You must tell them," Hal demanded as Uncle Nat closed their door. "They'd listen to you. She can't have stolen the necklace, because I was with her in the generator room."

"If we tell them you were with Marlene, then they'll say you lied in your interview and think you're guilty as well." Uncle Nat shook his head. "And what on earth was she doing in Milo's compartment?"

"Looking for clues," said Hal. "I would have been in there, too, but I was too scared to climb out the window."

"Well, thank goodness you were. Or you might both be locked up in that luggage cage."

"Everything's going wrong." Hal flopped down on the sofa, covering his face with his hands. "Milo isn't even the thief."

Uncle Nat fell silent, waiting for Hal to go on.

"That note we found? It was a love letter. Milo's in love with

Sierra, but they're trying to keep it a secret. Lucy's been their go-between, hiding notes in books in the library."

Uncle Nat sat down at his desk. The lakes and trees flashing past were replaced by houses and parking lots as they approached the outskirts of Manchester. "We'll be in Crewe in a few hours," he said.

Hal's heart jumped at the mention of his hometown.

"Given everything that's happened"—Uncle Nat looked at him—"I wonder if I shouldn't call your dad and ask him to come and get you."

"No!" Hal felt the world falling away from under him.

"You never asked to be dragged into any of this, Hal. You didn't even want to set foot on this train."

"But I'm glad I did. Please don't call Dad." He stood up. "I don't want to leave the Highland Falcon, not till the end. Please! Lenny's my friend—I have to help her. Dad's got enough to worry about with Mom and the baby. Please, Uncle Nat?"

Uncle Nat hesitated. "All right. But no more sneaking about in other people's rooms."

Hal nodded. "I promise."

Uncle Nat shook his head. "How on earth are we going to help Mohanjit and Lenny?"

"By finding the real thief," Hal said, pulling out his sketch-book and putting it on the desk. "All the jigsaw puzzle pieces are in here. I know it. We've got to be able to figure out who the real Magpie is."

As the train clattered through the outskirts of Manchester, slowing to a crawl for the waving crowds in Piccadilly station,

Hal and his uncle talked through what they knew about the day the necklace was stolen.

"It's no good," Hal said. "We're going around in circles."

"Maybe we should take a break. There's a royal reception at Crewe that I have to cover. Do you want to come?"

"Why didn't we stop in Manchester for a royal reception? That's a much bigger city than Crewe."

"Crewe is an important railway town." Uncle Nat tutted. "Surely you know that. You live there."

Hal shook his head.

"It's between London, Manchester, Birmingham, and Liverpool. If you think of the railways spread out over the country like a spiderweb"—he held up his balled fist—"then Crewe is like the knot at the center that ties them all together. The town grew up around the station. The railway works, the marshalling yards, factories, and houses for the workers to live in. If it weren't for railways, your home would be a field."

Hal blinked. He'd spent his whole life in Crewe and hadn't known it was a railway town.

"So do you want to come to a party to celebrate your hometown? There'll be cake."

"I can't go to a party while Lenny's locked in the luggage cage . . . This might sound strange, but I'd like to find somewhere quiet to sit so I can draw. Drawing helps me think."

"It doesn't sound strange at all, Hal. There are lots of different ways of thinking." Uncle Nat pulled on his jacket. "Why don't you go to the observation car? You'll be able to see the party from there, and I can slip you a piece of cake if you get hungry."

***

Hal entered the observation car, clutching his sketchbook and pen, and found a seat concealed from view by a wide-leafed tropical plant. He needed to slow his brain right down, and drawing had that effect on him. Jumping to conclusions was how he and Lenny had come to believe Milo was the Magpie. Thinking slowly was the key.

Hal opened his sketchbook to a double blank page, flattening the spine with the palm of his hand.

The Highland Falcon steamed into Crewe. The sandy bricks and lattice of white iron girders Hal had known all his life were strung with red-white-and-blue bunting. He felt a peculiar wrench to be surrounded by so much that was familiar, while sitting in the Highland Falcon—experiencing a world from the past. It was like being in a time machine.

Outside, a choir of children was singing "The Runaway Train." Hal thought of his mom and wondered if she'd had the baby yet. Closing his eyes, he fiercely wished that they were both okay. He opened them again and watched the guests disembark. He heard the cheer for the prince and princess, and his wrist twitched, his pen skittering across the page: the hard lines of the Crewe signage appeared; the soft lines of people. As his pen moved, his mind opened like a flower, and he began seeing patterns.

Ernest White, standing with a cup of tea, back bowed, biting into a piece of Battenberg—four small squares of cake making up a bigger square. What did Hal know about the old man with the half-moon glasses? Ernest had retired after dedicating his life to managing the royal train. He knew the Highland Falcon

178

inside out and the habits of the royal family. He could still have a key to the royal compartment.

Hal drew a key with a question mark inside it. The man had no obvious motive other than money. He loved the steam train. Hal smiled, remembering the fluffy microphone he'd clamped to the window in the dining car to record the chuffing of the train. It didn't seem so odd

to him now. *The microphone!* It had been in the dining car all this time. What if Ernest had recorded an important clue? He sketched a fluffy microphone by Ernest's head.

He looked up. Then there was Lucy Meadows, a pear shape, eating a fairy cake beside a banner for the Women's Institute. Hal liked Lucy. She had a warm smile and blushed easily, but she wasn't a pushover. Could she have stolen the necklace as a way to escape working for Sierra?

Fluffy microphone

Hal drew Sierra in elongated rectangles, a pea-sized head with big hair. She posed beside the mayor of Crewe, her lips pursed as if she were about to kiss him. Isaac, a solid square, knelt down in front of them with his camera. Sierra grabbed Milo's arm, dragging him into the picture. Hal smiled as he drew the brooding Milo, hooded eyes and snarling lip. Their secret love was taking its toll.

Isaac's camera

Sierra is vain, he thought, drawing a row of ticks to make the frilly hem of her skirt, *but why would she steal a necklace that belonged to her friend?* He sketched in the princess, standing on the other side of the mayor: a small upside-down equilateral triangle above a larger one the right way up, an oval face, long straight hair and a hat the shape of Saturn. Sierra's career was soaring. Would she really risk her fame for a necklace she could never wear in public?

The Pickles were seated together, two dumplings on a bench by the brick wall of the waiting room. Mr. Pickle looked angry. Hal drew the collar of his shirt and an enormous beet for his  head, with tiny eyes and a flat line for a mouth. Would a multimillionaire entrepreneur gain anything by stealing the Atlas Diamond?

Lydia Pickle was eating the cake off her husband's plate. Like a series of balloons, she was all bosoms, bottom, and big hair. She smiled at everyone and said things without thinking, but Hal thought she was funny and kind. She'd been the first to lose jewelry to the Magpie, which made her an unlikely suspect, and she didn't seem smart enough to mastermind the stealing of the Atlas Diamond.

The prince, an upright, chiseled man with an easy smile, was hardly going to steal his own wife's necklace. Lady Lansbury was standing beside him, immaculately dressed in a navy gown covered in twinkling crystals. Hal drew a bell shape, focusing on the accessories dripping from her ears, neck, and wrists. It was unlikely a woman so wealthy would steal the Atlas Diamond, and he couldn't imagine her hiding in the princess's wardrobe.

Baron Essenbach had legs like saplings and a chest like a bass clef. He stood beside Uncle Nat, admiring the Highland Falcon. The baron was a wealthy man and long-standing friend of the royal family. He was an unlikely suspect.

And then there was his uncle. Hal drew the looping infinity sign of his tortoiseshell glasses. Uncle Nat had no alibi. He'd been standing beside Lydia Pickle when her brooch went missing. Hal remembered him mentioning being at the Duchess of Kent's gala where the Magpie had struck before the  Highland Falcon began her journey. Hal lifted his pen, rolling it over his index finger. Could Uncle Nat be the Magpie? Surely not . . .

Glancing across the page, Hal realized the party was one person short. Rowan Buck was missing. Since the incident at Balmoral, Lady Lansbury hadn't let the dogs out at public events. The gentleman-in-waiting was probably with them in their compartment. Hal realized he had never drawn Rowan—always preferring to sketch the dogs. He drew a man with a blank face holding five taut leashes, at the ends of which he sketched ten triangle ears.

He had considered every one of the guests. Could it be someone else? Gordon, perhaps? Or Amy? Hal twirled his pen between his fingers, then circled the fluffy microphone beside Ernest White.

Perhaps his recording would produce a clue.

CHAPTER TWENTY-SIX

SOUND AND VISION

"Mr. White, could I talk to you?" Hal had been waiting for Ernest to get back on the train.

"Of course, Harrison. How can I help you?"

"You know the recordings you make with your microphone in the dining car? Have you listened back to any of them?"

"A few." Ernest gave him a watery-eyed smile. "And the Highland Falcon sounds tremendous."

The guard's whistle signaled that all the guests were aboard, and the dining-car doors were closed.

"Do you know, every time I hear a train whistle, I think of the prince's father?"

"Really? I wanted to ask you—"

"When he was five, the Highland Falcon was at Wolferton station—in Norfolk—and the prince was seeing off Queen Mary, his great-grandmother."

"That's interesting . . . I was wondering—"

"He asked the guard if he could look at his whistle, and as soon as he was given it, the rascal gave it a great blow, and the

182

train set off by mistake. The poor guard had to run and jump on the moving train, and he never got his whistle back." Ernest chuckled. "Little rapscallion!"

"Your recorder," pressed Hal. "Is it running all the time?"

"I have two machines. I swap them over every six hours. I have a listen and enter the date and time in my book, and which part of the route the recording is from. If you come to my room, I'll show you."

Ernest walked briskly in front of him. Hal noticed that despite his years, the old train manager had impressive rail legs, his body swaying with the motion of the train. "Have you noticed your microphone picking up conversations in the dining car?"

"That's not my intent," said Ernest sternly. "The microphone is placed *outside* the window, but some people are horrendously loud."

"Like Mr. Pickle?" Hal grinned.

"Yes—that bilious baboon has ruined the sound of steam pushing pistons on a number of occasions." Ernest rolled his eyes. "He complains loudly, and he boasts about Grailax, trying to get people to invest in his awful company." He lowered his voice. "When he told Lady Lansbury, and then the baron, that he was having cash-flow problems, it was hard not to smile."

"I thought he was rich."

"Rich people can have money troubles, too, you know."

They'd reached Ernest's compartment. The old man entered and sat on his sofa.

"I miss my old place in the service car. It wasn't much, but it suited me."

"I was hoping you might have heard something on your recorder that would help clear Lenny and Mr. Singh—a clue, maybe."

"I don't think so." Ernest pointed to a small black book on his desk. "That's where I write everything down. You can borrow it if you like. You're welcome to listen to the recordings, but it would take days."

Hal picked up the book and opened it. Each page was divided into four columns: *Date*, *Time*, *Route*, and *Notes*.

"Have you heard anything that Lady Lansbury's gentleman-in-waiting has said?" Hal asked.

"You can hear Lady Lansbury talking to him twice, but Mr. Buck is too quiet. I must say, for a woman of such high

Date	Time	Route	Notes
Aug 28th	7.30am	Forth Bridge	Bridge irons sing, whistle sounds
Aug 28th	9.30am	Near Montrose	Sluicing water, refilling at speed
Aug 28th	11.00am	Deeside Line	Under good steam

standing, she uses some ripe language to describe those dogs of hers."

"Thanks, Mr. White. You've been a great help," Hal said.

"Anything to help Mohanjit. He's an honorable man," Ernest said. He pointed at the black book. "I will be wanting that back. It contains precious information."

"I promise to take good care of it." Hal went to the door. "I don't suppose you know where Isaac went?"

"I believe Mr. Adebayo returned to his compartment for batteries."

On his way to Isaac's compartment, Hal thought he heard the sound of a dog whining and stopped to listen. He realized it was actually a woman crying. The sobs were coming from the bathroom at the end of the corridor. He wondered if he should knock but decided it was best not to intrude and hurried past.

Isaac's door was open. He greeted Hal with a smile.

"Harrison Beck," he said. "Come in. You are just the man I wanted to see."

Glossy pictures were attached by bulldog clips to string zig-zagging across the room. Hal spotted one of himself glaring at Mr. Pickle.

"Sorry about the mess," Isaac said, gathering a bundle of old photographs from the floor and handing them to Hal. "Could you take these to your uncle? He asked me to dig out a few historic pictures of the royal train for his article. That top one is for you."

Hal took the bundle and looked at a black-and-white photo of a group of people standing in front of the Highland Falcon at Ballater station.

"It's from a royal Christmas nearly twenty years ago," Isaac said.

A young Ernest White stood proudly at the picture's edge, in the uniform Gordon Goulde now wore. Next to him was Gladys from Balmoral. And in the middle, a boy about Hal's age stood smiling at his grandmother, the queen.

"It's the prince, wearing my awful itchy blazer and bow tie!"

Isaac laughed. "Not only must you suffer the indignity of wearing another man's clothes, but fashion that is twenty years out of date."

"Is that Lady Lansbury?"

"And her husband, the count," said Isaac. "That's Beatrice and Terrence, their children." He tutted. "It was sad when Count Arundel died. The family fell apart."

"What happened?"

"The count lived life to excess, throwing lavish parties whenever he could. His children were the same." He pursed his lips, choosing his words carefully. "They broke some laws and are now paying for their crimes."

"Poor Lady Lansbury."

"She's made of strong stuff, that woman. A tsunami couldn't knock her over. Anyway, tell your uncle if he needs more pictures, I have plenty."

"I had a question about the Atlas Diamond," Hal said. "Do you have pictures of the real one *and* the fake one? I thought I might be able to spot the difference, work out when the switch happened."

"The police had the same idea." Isaac shook his head. "Whoever made that fake was an artist. They really know their stuff." Isaac opened his laptop, revealing a grid of images. "I'm not sure there's anything to find. But, here—take a look."

Hal clicked on a picture of himself getting out of the black car outside Balmoral and enlarged it. He scrolled through the images quickly, stopping when he found the first picture of the princess. She had a hand on Sierra's shoulder, the two of them laughing at the excitement with the Samoyeds. The Atlas Diamond was splitting light and scattering rainbows. Hal flicked further ahead, to a shot of the royal couple coming into lunch, to another of them getting into their car, boarding the train, greeting crowds at Aberdeen. But Isaac was right. Nothing he saw seemed suspicious—and the necklace looked the same in every single picture.

CHAPTER TWENTY-SEVEN

DRAWING CONCLUSIONS

A patchwork of butter-yellow and avocado-green Shropshire farmland was flying past the window as Hal entered the compartment.

"Isaac asked me to bring you these. They're for your article."

"Thanks." Uncle Nat took the pictures. "How did the drawing go?"

"I had some ideas." Hal held up Ernest's black book. "I thought Ernest may have picked up a clue on his recordings, and I dropped in on Isaac to see if there was a difference in the photos of the real Atlas Diamond and the fake." He sighed. "But there wasn't."

"There's been another development in the case, although I don't know what it means." Uncle Nat looked somber. "Before we left Crewe, Inspector Clyde produced a bracelet and asked who it belonged to. No one seemed to recognize it. It remains unclaimed. It was discovered in the Highland Falcon's tender, hidden among the coal. The detective chief inspector seems to think it's proof that Mohanjit and Lenny are guilty."

"Did it look like this?" Hal opened his sketchbook and held up his drawing of the bracelet from Milo's compartment.

"Yes! But . . ."

"Lenny saw a bracelet in Milo's room. I drew what she described."

"It's an astonishing likeness." Uncle Nat blinked. "But then, why didn't Milo claim the bracelet? Inspector Clyde was most put out when no one came forward."

"It must be Sierra's. They're keeping their relationship a secret." Hal looked down at his drawing. "If the bracelet was in Milo's room when Lenny was in there, and then she was caught and taken straight to the luggage cage, then this picture is *proof* she couldn't have taken the bracelet and hidden it in the tender. Mr. Singh couldn't have done it, either." Hal looked up at his uncle. "The Magpie must have planted the bracelet in the tender to frame the Singhs! I need to show the detective my drawing."

"Inspector Clyde is unlikely to admit an undatable drawing as evidence of their innocence, Hal."

"No," said Hal, sinking onto the sofa. "I guess not." His face fell. He'd followed every lead he could think of and had still found nothing to help Lenny.

***

Cheerful strings of bunting fluttered past the window as they chuffed into Shrewsbury station, and Hal felt sadness envelop him like a scratchy blanket. He hated thinking of Lenny locked up in that luggage cage. He hoped she wasn't frightened.

"I'm no good at being a detective," he said.

"That not true, Hal," Uncle Nat reassured him. "I've seen you instinctively acting like an investigative journalist. You're asking good questions and noticing important details. You're seeing things no one else is."

"But it's getting me nowhere." Hal half-heartedly punched the sofa cushion.

"Two heads are better than one." Uncle Nat pulled down the blinds. "Why don't you pretend I'm a stranger who knows nothing about what's happened on this train, and you tell me everything as you see it? It might help to say everything out loud, rather than have it all swirling about in your head."

"Okay."

"I'll put the desk up, and we can sit on the floor. Different place, different head space."

Hal sat cross-legged on the thick blue carpet and laid his sketchbook and Ernest White's black book in front of him. Uncle Nat sat opposite, placing the railway map between them.

"Start with the facts," Uncle Nat said, picking up his fountain pen. Hal noticed he had a knobbly callus on his middle finger where the pen rested.

Uncle Nat opened his journal. "What do we actually *know*?"

"The first thing I noticed was the newspaper story about a thief who had stolen a ruby ring at a charity gala." Hal took out the torn-off front page from the back of his book and laid it out on the floor. "It says the thief has stolen other things in the past, all from fancy houses or at posh parties." He looked at his uncle. "Then jewelry aboard the Highland Falcon started going missing. I thought this thief"—he pointed at the article—"might be aboard the train. But it could be someone else, or a copycat pretending to be them."

"Excellent." Uncle Nat wrote this down in his journal.

"I don't know enough about the other robberies to draw connections," Hal said, "but you said you were at the Duchess of Kent's charity gala where the ruby ring went missing . . ."

"I was." Uncle Nat nodded.

"And so were the baron, his son Milo, and Sierra Knight—who brought her assistant, Lucy. The Pickles were there, too, and made a great show of bidding for everything at the charity auction without going as far as trying to win any of the prizes. Lady Lansbury put in an appearance, and Isaac told me he was there taking pictures, although I didn't see him. It was a huge affair."

"The first theft on the train was Lydia Pickle's brooch, which had to have been taken by someone in the observation car on that first evening." Hal opened his sketchbook, pointing to the picture. "A few minutes after this moment, she said she'd lost it. Either it fell off, or it was stolen by the Magpie. If it had fallen off, it would've been found by now—which means that the Magpie must be one of the people who was in the room."

"Who else was there?"

"All of the guests, Gordon Goulde, Amy, and Lenny."

"Lenny?"

"She was hiding under the drinks trolley."

"I see. Who *wasn't* there?"

"Rowan Buck—and all other train staff."

"Right." Uncle Nat made a note.

"The next crime was the theft of Lady Lansbury's earrings," said Hal. "We know they were taken from her compartment that same night, but we don't know anything else about the crime."

"Very well. Crime three—the big one—the mysterious theft of the Atlas Diamond necklace. We've gathered from the police that the princess didn't take the necklace off until she got into her compartment as the train pulled away from Ballater."

"Hadrian was standing guard by her door all the way to Aberdeen," Hal said. "I saw him. He was there until she left the room."

Uncle Nat tapped his fountain pen against his lip. "So, whoever switched the necklace for the fake must have been hiding in the compartment before the princess went inside—and they must have *stayed* inside unseen all that time."

"Lots of the guests have alibis. I saw Ernest and the baron playing billiards. Lucy was in the library reading a book, and Isaac was in the observation car taking photographs. I saw Lady Lansbury talking to Rowan in the gentlemen's lounge. Ooh, and that was where Amy brought me the scones—so we can rule her out, too."

"If we cross out everyone you saw from the list of people who could have taken Mrs. Pickle's brooch, where does that leave us?"

Hal flicked back to the first drawing, mentally scribbling out the faces of the people with alibis for the journey from Ballater to Aberdeen.

"Milo and Sierra don't officially have alibis, but I think that's because they were with each other. That leaves four people: Gordon Goulde, Mr. and Mrs. Pickle . . . and you."

"Marvelous. Do me first. I'm rather taken by the idea of being an international jewel thief."

"Well, you say you were here, having a nap, but I left you before the princess got on the train. You could have run along to the royal compartment, somehow opened the door, and hidden in the wardrobe."

"I could have." Uncle Nat nodded. "I have absolutely no alibi."

"You were also standing next to Lydia Pickle when her brooch went missing."

"It's looking very bad for me, isn't it?" Uncle Nat chuckled. "Anything else?"

"There's the bracelet . . . ," Hal said, his voice trailing off.

"What about it?"

"You could've broken into Milo's compartment, not knowing Lenny was hiding in there, and taken the bracelet. And then, after I left, you could have heard the police arresting Lenny and seized the opportunity to throw the bracelet into the tender—" Hal caught his breath, staring at his uncle. "You could have done all of the crimes," he said in a small voice.

"And what would my motive be?"

"Er . . . money? Because it can't really be true you can make a living writing about trains." Hal felt sick. He wasn't sure he wanted to be a detective anymore.

"Brilliant! So, I'm the prime suspect." Uncle Nat looked untroubled, which reassured Hal. If he was the thief, then surely he'd be worried. "Now let's consider the others."

"Um, Steven Pickle definitely didn't take the bracelet, because he was with me." He looked at his uncle. "Although he has a strong motive for stealing the Atlas Diamond. He's desperate for money."

"Really?" Uncle Nat blinked. "How do you know that?"

"Ernest has recordings of him asking Lady Lansbury and the baron to invest in Grailax."

Uncle Nat sat back. "You're a better journalist than me!"

"But I don't think he's the Magpie. Can you imagine Steven Pickle hiding in the princess's wardrobe? Darting out and switching the real for the fake?" Hal shook his head. "He stomps everywhere, has hands like hams, and he doesn't know how to whisper."

Uncle Nat laughed. "To be honest, I can't imagine *anyone* hiding in the wardrobe all that time—but I get your point."

"It can't be Lydia Pickle, either, because if she were planning to steal the Atlas Diamond, she'd be crazy to steal her own brooch first and make such a fuss about there being a thief."

"So, really, I'm the only person with the opportunity and motive to have committed all the thefts," Uncle Nat summarized. "The next question, of course, is where have I hidden the jewels?"

"I don't know." Hal flicked through the pages of his sketchbook. "The police have been through the train with a fine-toothed comb and a pack of sniffer dogs." He sat back and scratched his head.

"Why don't you ponder it over supper?" Uncle Nat got to his feet. "I don't know about you, but all this investigating is making me hungry. I say we go to the dining car and ban talk of the Highland Falcon Thief until we're back in the compartment."

"But what if I can't find proof you're not the Magpie?" Hal asked nervously. "Aren't you worried?"

"Not a bit," said Uncle Nat, helping Hal to his feet. "I have absolute faith in you. Now come on—let's eat."

***

After dinner, Hal changed into his pajamas and clambered into his bunk with his sketchbook. Isaac's picture fell out of the back, and he looked at it, smiling, glad to have an image of the Highland Falcon. He pushed it back inside the book. *If I were the thief, aboard this train, where would I hide the jewels?* He gazed out the window as the train pulled away from Shrewsbury, trundling through a junction to make its way down the Welsh Marches line, heading for the south coast.

Where is the Atlas Diamond? Flicking through the pictures in his book, he couldn't help feeling he was missing something that was staring him in the face. Time was slipping away one chuff at a time. *Harrison Beck, Harrison Beck*, the clacking rails called his name. *Harrison Beck, Harrison Beck.* He couldn't let Lenny and her dad go to prison. *Harrison Beck, Harrison Beck.* He imagined his friend in the luggage cage, hugging her knees. *Harrison Beck.* He saw Ernest with his microphone trying to catch the chuffs; Milo desperately writing love letters; Uncle Nat in handcuffs; Bailey with sad blue eyes; Sierra Knight stealing a lipstick from Inspector Clyde, who was too busy playing with Penny Mouse to notice.

"Wake up, Hal." Uncle Nat was shaking him gently, and sunlight was streaming in through the window. "It's morning."

"Oh no! I didn't mean to go to sleep." Hal sat bolt upright, pushing back his covers. His sketchbook fell to the floor, its pages splayed. "There's not much time left. We arrive in London today."

"Calm yourself." Uncle Nat looked at one of the wrist-watches on his left arm. "There are nine whole hours till we arrive in Paddington, and it's three in the morning in New York. Half the world is still sleeping."

Hal wriggled out of his pajamas, pulling on his jeans and T-shirt.

"We're in Swansea, about to turn around." Uncle Nat went to the sink and splashed water on his face. As he dabbed his face dry with the hand towel, there was a knock at the door. He put his glasses on and went to answer it.

Amy stood on the threshold holding a large silver tray.

"Breakfast!" she said brightly, coming in and setting it down on the desk.

"We didn't order breakfast," Uncle Nat said.

"Boiled eggs for Harrison Beck. Kippers and toast for Nathaniel Bradshaw, with a pot of coffee and orange juice," Amy said, lifting the silver covers from their plates.

"Well, that does look rather good." Uncle Nat leaned over the tray, closing his eyes as he breathed in.

Amy looked at Hal with wide eyes. She stared at the boiled eggs—and then back at him—gave a tiny nod of her head and promptly left.

"How odd," Uncle Nat said, forking a bit of kipper onto a corner of toast and popping it in his mouth. "Mmmm."

Hal lifted his plate onto his lap. The two boiled eggs sat in two tiny steam-train egg cups. He cracked the top off one and saw a perfectly sunny runny yolk. He brought his silver spoon down on the second egg, and it collapsed. It was hollow. He frowned, lifting the battered shell. Inside, he found a rolled-up piece of paper.

"There's a note in my egg!"

Uncle Nat stopped pouring the coffee. "I beg your pardon?"

Hal pulled the note out and read it to himself:

Hal,

Milo isn't the Magpie. Someone broke into his room while I was hidden in the drawer under the sofa. I tried to get out after they'd gone, but the police were in the corridor. They've locked me in the luggage

cage and taken my fingerprints. They say my dad
will go to prison. You have to help me. I'm getting
scared, and something in here smells really bad.

Lenny

"Hal? Are you okay?"

The mess of clues that had seemed as scattered as children
in a playground were coming together in patterns. The whistle
blew. Lines gathered and crisscrossed and met at points. They
made shapes. They made *sense*. Hal looked at his uncle.

"I know who did it."

CHAPTER TWENTY-EIGHT

ARRESTING BEHAVIOR

"I need to get to Lenny." Hal pulled on his sweater, jammed his feet in his sneakers, and grabbed his sketchbook. "Don't try to stop me."

"I wouldn't dream of it," Uncle Nat said. "But there are police officers guarding the royal carriage, the luggage cage, and the footplate. They'll never let you through."

"I have to try."

"I'll come with you." Uncle Nat knocked back his coffee and stood up.

"My plan won't work if you're with me."

"Oh, right." Uncle Nat sat back down, looking crestfallen. "Well, if I can do anything . . ."

But Hal was already running to the dining car. He peeped in. Inspector Clyde was seated at the near end with her back to the door. He sidestepped into the hot and noisy kitchen, where Amy was standing by the coffee machine.

"What are you doing in here?" Amy hissed, as she frothed milk in a silver jug.

"I need to get to Lenny," Hal said.

Amy shook her head. "Impossible."

"You did it. You brought me a note."

"I'm allowed to take her breakfast, lunch, and dinner," Amy said, removing the jug and wiping the steam nozzle with a cloth. "But I'm supervised by an officer the whole time. This morning, I took her boiled eggs. She put the note in the egg and winked at me. I read it and brought it to you."

"You're a good friend. Lots of grown-ups wouldn't do that."

"Who wants to be a grown-up?" Amy shrugged. "Not me, that's for sure."

"I think I can prove Lenny and her dad are innocent, but I have to get into the luggage cage. Is there another way in?"

"No, they load in luggage from the outside door, but it's been locked the whole trip. The only accessible door is the inside door, and Sergeant Prattle sits right outside it."

"Guess it's going to have to be plan B, then."

"What's plan B?"

Hal marched to the table where Inspector Clyde was sitting. She looked up at him.

"Can I help you?"

Hal thrust both his hands forward. "I'm here to confess. I'm Marlene Singh's accomplice. We stole the necklace together, and I'm turning myself in. You must arrest me at once."

"Indeed?" Inspector Clyde pursed her lips. "Well, this is very serious. Come with me."

She grabbed Hal by the wrist, leading him out of the dining

car. His heart beat wildly, but his plan was working. Inspector Clyde suddenly stopped. Hal bumped into her as she knocked at his own door.

"Your nephew is making trouble, Mr. Bradshaw," she said as Uncle Nat opened the door. "He's told me a load of nonsense about being an accomplice and wanting to be arrested." She let go of Hal's wrist. "Now, I like a joke, but the boy doesn't seem to understand the severity of this situation." She fixed Hal with a cool stare. "If you really want to be arrested, I'll have a squad car waiting at the next station to take you away to prison."

"My word, I am sorry," said Uncle Nat. "He's been cooped up on this train too long. Cabin fever, probably. It won't happen again."

"Be sure it doesn't." Inspector Clyde eyeballed Hal. "If I catch you anywhere near that luggage cage, I'll throw you off the train myself."

Uncle Nat closed the door and spun around. "Well, that was a bold move."

Hal sighed. "Amy says it's impossible to get to the luggage cage from inside the train. It's too heavily guarded." He went over to the map of the route on the wall. "Are we stopping for coal and water anywhere?"

"At Bristol," Uncle Nat replied, pointing over his shoulder. "We'll refuel at Temple Meads station, then take the Great Western Mainline back to London." He moved his finger along the route. "We'll go through Box Tunnel, one of the longest in the country, and over the Wharncliffe Viaduct—"

"How long are we going to be at Bristol?"

"A fair while. It's the last formal function before London.

Why? What are you planning?"

Hal looked at the route map and took a deep breath. "I think I can prove Lenny and Mr. Singh are innocent, but I'll need help."

"Of course, Hal. What do you need?"

Hal explained, and Uncle Nat's eyes widened.

"The only way into the luggage cage is from the outside," Hal finished. "And I have to do it at Bristol."

"But no one's going to let you anywhere near that end of the train," Uncle Nat said. "They'll be guarding it like hawks."

"Maybe," said Hal with a grin. "But there is one person they'll let near it."

***

The Highland Falcon puffed triumphantly under the grand arches of Bristol Temple Meads. A gathering of onlookers waved and cheered as she pulled alongside the platform.

"Such a beautiful station," said Isaac, taking a photograph from the veranda of the observation car.

"It was the first station designed by Isambard Kingdom Brunel," said Hal. "He built most of England's railways. I read that in my uncle's book."

"You're a chip off the Bradshaw block, aren't you?" Isaac said. "Now, grab that tripod and let's go."

Isaac jumped down onto the platform as the train pulled to a halt, and Hal followed. Isaac started snapping pictures, making a show of photographing the carriages, the crowd, and the architecture of the station.

"It's nice having an assistant." Isaac lifted a camera from around Hal's neck. "Can you pass me that lens? Thanks. If you ever want a job, get your uncle to call me."

They worked as a double act: Hal setting up the tripod, while Isaac adjusted his camera and focused the shots, moving along the platform as they went. Soon the glistening claret engine was in view, and Isaac photographed the beautiful A4 Pacific gleaming in the August sunshine.

Hal spotted Joey walking beside the boiler and checking the engine.

"Can we get close to Joey?" Hal whispered.

"Sure." Isaac strode toward the fireman, snapping away. A policewoman stepped forward to block their path. Isaac lowered his camera. "I'm afraid the royal family don't want the official photographs to feature police officers." He smiled apologetically. "I need to capture the fireman working on the engine. It's the last time he'll ever do it, and I need that photo."

The policewoman stepped aside, and Isaac strode past the engine compartment. Hal hurried after him and caught a glimpse of Lenny's dad on the footplate, handcuffed to a policeman.

"Mr. Bray, would you mind if I photographed you?" Isaac called out.

"Nope," Joey replied. "You do your job. I'll do mine."

"Hal, pass me the Canon 5D."

Unhooking the camera from around his neck, Hal walked round to stand in front of Isaac, managing to place himself less than three feet from Joey.

"Joey," Hal said, his voice low and urgent, "I know who took the necklace, but I need proof."

Isaac checked the light with a handheld device and framed the shot with his fingers, drawing attention away from Hal, who remained motionless, lips barely moving.

"Mmm-hmmm," Joey muttered, rubbing an oily rag along a metal crank.

"I'm going to clear Mr. Singh's and Lenny's names."

Joey looked at him, clear blue eyes in a craggy face smeared with coal dust. "His fire's gone out," he said, his voice cracking.

"The evidence I need is in the luggage car with Lenny." Hal's eyes flicked to the police officer, but she was looking at Isaac. "I've tried to get in there, but it's heavily guarded. Is there a way in from the outside?"

Joey shook his head.

"What about the skylight?"

Joey's eyebrows shot up. "You'd have to be crazy."

"I could get through it—I'm certain I could."

Joey bent down so that his face was obscured.

"There's a ladder that goes up the side of the service car and over the top of the train. The boys use it for cleaning the carriages. You can reach it from the tender corridor . . . But, Harrison, you can't climb it while the train's moving—you won't be able to cling on. It's too dangerous."

"What about when the train's going super slow? Through a station—like Bath Spa."

"I suppose . . . it's possible."

"Then tell Mr. Singh to go as slow as he can for as long as possible through Bath Spa."

Hal turned away before Joey could talk him out of it. He handed Isaac his other camera. "Isaac, I need to get into the tender corridor. Can you get me near the loco?"

Isaac nodded. "Stay here until I call for you." Then he tailed Joey as the fireman adjusted a giant hose that snaked up into the water tank. "Oh dear!" he exclaimed, shaking his camera. "Hal!" he called over his shoulder. "Battery's dead. I need a new one."

Hal obediently scurried to Isaac's elbow, offering him what he hoped was a battery pack from the black case. Isaac unhooked the two cameras hanging around Hal's neck, pulling them over his own head, and leaned against the tender, looking around as he fitted the battery to the back of his camera.

"Coast is clear," Isaac said quietly. "Go now. Quick!"

Hal ducked into the gap between the engine and the service car and slipped into the dark tender corridor.

CHAPTER TWENTY-NINE

BELT AND BRACE YOURSELF

he tender corridor was pitch-black. Hal could hear the rushing sound of water filling the tank. His heart thumped at the thought of what he was about to do. Yesterday, the idea of climbing out of a window had made him feel sick. Today, he would have to climb onto the roof of a moving train.

Today is different. Lenny needs me.

Uncle Nat had said it would take about fifteen minutes for the Highland Falcon to get to Bath. He had to hope that no one decided to go through the tender corridor in that time, or he'd be caught. The gushing sound stopped, and there was a bang as the hose was pulled from the water tank. Hal swallowed, trying to reassure his jumping heart as his left leg jiggled up and down.

I won't fall off, he told himself. *Mr. Singh will drive slowly. I'll cling on tight.* His heart boomed in his ears. *I can do this. I will do this.*

Standing in the dark, time stretched out forever. Hal wished he had a watch. How was he going to know when they were approaching Bath? He'd have to count the seconds. His chest felt tight. A shock ran through him as the Highland Falcon coughed out a burst of steam, and the tender jolted forward. The wheels beneath him squeaked as they turned, and the train pulled away from Bristol.

As they gathered speed, the tender rocked. Hal braced himself against the walls. His hands were sweaty. He imagined his grip on the ladder slipping and wiped his palms against his trousers. He staggered. It was hard to balance in the dark.

He counted the seconds, adding up to minutes. When he reached what he thought must be about fifteen minutes, Hal pulled open the rear door of the tender. He saw trees and track whipping past. He looked at the ladder. It was to the right of the door into the service car. If Amy was right, there would be a police officer on the other side of that door. He had to be quiet, as well as careful. Without allowing himself to think, he sprang lightly across the gap, reached out his right hand, and grabbed a rung of the ladder, hugging himself to it. He gasped with joyful relief . . . and then he began to climb, one rung to the next, his confidence building as he went.

At the top of the carriage, the ladder curved forward, hugging the roof, running alongside the skylights. Hal lifted his head and shoulders above the parapet, and, as if shoved from behind by a bully, the force of the wind over the top of the train knocked him forward, pushing his face into the roof, tipping him off-balance. His hands and feet fumbled to keep their grip. The wind roared in his ears, and he clung to the ladder for dear life.

Up here, the train didn't feel slow at all. He stared at the white roof, breathing hard. *You're doing great*, he told his hammering

heart. *Calm
down.* He carefully
slid his left arm between the
rungs of the ladder, underneath one and
over the next, gripping on as securely as he could.

Then he reached down with his right hand, unbuckled his
belt, and fastened it around one of the ladder rungs. It held him
there, steady, and he could relax his grip as the train slid through
the outskirts of a town, houses gathering around the tracks.

Unwinding his arm, Hal eased himself forward, pushing along
the ladder with his feet as far as the belt would let him. Then he
secured his arm, reached down to untie his belt, straightened his
legs, and fastened the belt over the next rung. Like a caterpillar,

one rung at a time, he made his way forward. He thought of films where heroes ran over the roofs of speeding trains. They seemed ridiculous now.

The skylights were evenly spaced along the roof. The first one overlooked the generator room. The second was blacked out. His arms ached so hard, they'd gone to jelly. He moved another rung forward, squinting through the soot and smoke and gritting his teeth as his yellow jacket whipped about. He looked around, searching for signs that they were nearing Bath.

The track ran on raised ground, the same height as the rooftops of passing houses. Trees and telephone poles catapulted past. A child in an upstairs bedroom window spotted him and pointed, then was gone. He moved another rung forward. The shrill peal of the train's whistle almost made Hal lose his grip. It blew once, twice, three times—and again for a long blast. Glancing over his shoulder, he saw a station approaching. It was too small to be Bath—and to his horror, beyond the station, he saw a low bridge.

Don't look. Just don't look, he told himself, closing his eyes and reaching forward. The third skylight seemed so far away. He had to reach it before the train reached the bridge. He undid his belt, giving up on safety, dragging himself forward rung by rung, trying not to think about losing his grip. He reached the skylight. Through it, he saw the top of Lenny's head. She was sitting on a pile of suitcases with her arms wrapped around her knees. He banged on the window. She lifted her head, leaping to her feet when she saw him, her eyes the size of saucers.

"*Help!*" Hal mouthed.

Lenny leaped across the room, throwing suitcases one on

top of another, scrambling on top of them to reach the skylight. Reaching up as high as she could, she flipped open a catch and pulled the window inward.

Hal threw his arms forward, clasping the base of the window and pulling himself through, plummeting to the luggage compartment floor as the whistle screamed and the train swept under the bridge.

CHAPTER THIRTY

A CAGE OF CASES

"Uuuuuuuuuuu," Hal moaned, winded by his landing.

Lenny threw her arms around him. "You came! You came!"

He gasped, trying to sit up. "What are you doing?"

"Hugging you." Lenny released him. "Did you get my note? What's happening? Can you smell that? It stinks in here."

Hal felt the train slow to a crawl. "Oh great—*now* we're coming into Bath Spa," he groaned. He'd mistimed everything and had nearly gotten himself killed.

There was a slamming sound, and Lenny shoved him hard. Hal found himself on the ground with a stack of cases being pushed on top of him.

"What's going on in there?"

Through a gap in the luggage pile, Hal spied Sergeant Prattle standing on the other side of the cage. He held his breath.

"Some cases fell over," Lenny replied, walking up to the iron mesh and pushing her face against it. "Please let me out of here," she begged. "I promise to be good."

211

"Sorry. Chief's orders."

Lenny stuck out her tongue. Sergeant Prattle grunted and left.

"Your chief stinks!"

Hal heard the carriage door shut.

Lenny pushed the cases off him. "I'm sorry. I didn't hurt you, did I?"

His whole body ached, but it wasn't from the cases. He shook his head.

"You climbed over the roof!" Lenny's face was a picture of awe. "Like an action hero. That's so *dangerous*."

"It is?" Hal felt a bit sick.

"*Yes!* I haven't got the guts to do that when the train's *moving*."

"I got your note." Hal felt dizzy and wanted Lenny to stop talking. He didn't feel like a hero. There was a good chance he might throw up. "I think I know who stole the necklace. I'm going to get you out of here and clear your dad's name."

Lenny sat back on her heels, biting her bottom lip. "Really?" She blinked back tears. "You wouldn't say it if you didn't mean it, would you?"

Hal shook his head and then fell backward a second time as Lenny threw her arms around him again.

"Ow! Get off!"

"Thank you—*thank you*." She shook him side to side with joy. "You're the best friend I've ever had in my whole life. I owe you—*big-time*." She pulled back. "Your baby sister's lucky. You'll make a pretty good big brother. Although next time, could you be a bit quicker?"

Hal laughed.

"Now tell me what we're doing." Lenny got to her feet.

"Where's the smell coming from?" asked Hal.

"Over there." She pointed at a tan suitcase with two gold buckles sitting on its own in the far corner. "I moved it as far away as possible."

Hal knelt down in front of it. "It's locked."

"Yeah," said Lenny, wrinkling her nose. "Thank goodness."

"We need to open it," said Hal. "Can you open the lock with something on your tool belt?"

"They took my tools, but . . ."

Lenny raised her boot and stamped the heel down on the first lock. The gold catch sprang open. She did it again on the second catch. Hal lifted the lid and gagged, immediately closing it. A revoltingly ripe smell leaked out.

"Eurgh!" Lenny covered her mouth and nose with her sweater. "What *is* that? It's *disgusting*!"

The case was full of small lumpy black bags tied shut. Hal tugged his sleeve over his hand and gingerly lifted one up between pinched fingers. "It's dog poo."

"*Dog poo?*"

"This explains everything," said Hal, reading the label. "Now we know where the princess's necklace is."

"We do?"

"Quick—we need to move all of this poo into a new suit-case . . . We need one that will shut."

"Why?" Lenny looked horrified.

"We're taking it with us."

"You're nuts," said Lenny, casting around for a suitcase that would open. "Why do you want to take the poo with you?"

"I'll explain in a minute." Hal opened a small blue suitcase and shook the clothes it contained out onto the floor. "Quick—let's swap the stuff."

"Ugh!"

"C'mon!" Hal snapped. "Our ride out of here will be arriving any minute."

Trying not to gag, they speedily transferred the bags of dog poo into the empty blue case.

"Now take off your boots," said Hal.

"Have you lost your marbles?"

"Just do it."

Lenny dropped to the floor, unlaced and yanked off her boots, while Hal stacked a pile of suitcases.

"Put your boots sticking out so it looks like you're sitting behind them," he said.

There was a rattle of keys. Hal fell to the floor. Grabbing a large suitcase with one hand and Lenny with the other, he pulled them toward the cage door, and they ducked behind the case.

"Grub's up!" Amy entered the corridor pushing a silver food trolley covered in a white tablecloth, accompanied by Sergeant Prattle.

Peeping over the case, Hal watched the detective pull a key on a wire from his belt and open the cage door.

"Aw, look—she's sulking!" Amy pointed at Lenny's boots.

Sergeant Prattle snorted. "Silly kid."

Amy lifted the tray of food. "Don't worry about me," she said. "It'll only take me a minute to give her her food."

"I can't leave you alone with her." Sergeant Prattle shook his head. "Inspector's orders. She might become violent."

"Aw." Amy smiled. "Are you protecting me from an eleven-year-old girl? How sweet."

Hal nudged Lenny forward, putting a finger to his lips, miming for her to get onto all fours. He held up a finger and listened.

The Highland Falcon let off a shrill whistle, and the carriage was plunged into darkness as the train disappeared into a tunnel.

"The trolley!" whispered Hal, his voice covered by the roaring dark. "Go!"

Lenny scrambled forward, and Hal followed right behind her. He lifted the tablecloth covering the food trolley, and Lenny clambered in, bringing her knees up to her chin to make room for him. Hal scrambled in backward, clutching the blue suitcase. It was a tight squeeze, but they just fit. Hal pulled the tablecloth back down as the train shot out of the tunnel and light returned to the carriage. Lenny gave Harrison a thumbs-up as Amy took the food to Lenny's boots, chatting away as if she were sitting there sulking. She wheeled the trolley out of the cage, and the police officer locked it.

"You all right down there?" Amy whispered, once they were a safe distance from the service car.

"You are a legend, Amy," Lenny hissed back. "And, Hal, you're a genius for using Box Tunnel like that."

"Uncle Nat said it's one of the longest tunnels in the country," whispered Hal. "I figured it would give us enough time."

Amy stopped the trolley momentarily as she passed through the kitchen.

"Are you ready, Gordon?" she asked.

"Now?" he replied.

"Yes, now," said Amy, pushing the trolley again.

"*What's happening?*" Lenny mouthed.

Hal put a finger to his lips and smiled.

An announcement came over the train's loudspeaker system as Amy pushed the trolley through the royal carriages, past Hadrian, and into the sleeping car.

"Would all passengers please gather in the dining car immediately," Gordon's voice said. "I repeat: would all passengers please gather in the dining car *immediately*."

Hal heard a door open.

"What does that detective want with us now?" Sierra complained.

"Perhaps she's found the necklace," Lucy suggested.

"Good," Sierra retorted. "I can't wait to get off this train."

"Get out of the way, woman!" Steven Pickle shouted.

"I'm afraid I can't move, sir," Amy replied. "There are people ahead of me."

The children grinned at each other as the passengers of the Highland Falcon grumbled, unaware they were hidden beneath the silver trolley. Hal peeped under the tablecloth as Amy pushed the trolley into the dining car, moving to the far end, and parked it by the private dining room.

"What is the meaning of this, Inspector Clyde?" Steven Pickle demanded.

"I was about to ask the same thing," the inspector declared. "I didn't call this meeting."

"What?" Gasps filled the room. "Then who did?"

Hal slipped out from under the trolley's tablecloth and stepped forward. "I did," he said.

Steven Pickle huffed, getting up to leave, but Uncle Nat pushed him back into his seat.

"I think you should stay and hear what Hal has to say."

"I know who the thief is," Hal said. "I know who stole the brooch, the earrings, the bracelet, and the princess's diamond necklace."

"We all do," Milo Essenbach said. "It was the train driver and his daughter."

"No, it wasn't." Hal shook his head. "The real thief is right here in this room."

CHAPTER THIRTY-ONE

THE END OF THE LINE

"**W**ell, this is a turnup for the books." Inspector Clyde smiled icily at Hal. "You've outsmarted a whole train of police have you, laddie?" She sat down. "Well, c'mon, then. You've got us all here now—let's hear it."

The carriage went quiet. Hal's hand went to his Saint Christopher.

"When I first got on the Highland Falcon, I read a newspaper article about a thief who'd been stealing jewels from high-society parties." He looked at Lydia Pickle. "Then Mrs. Pickle's brooch went missing."

She winked at him.

"I thought the thefts might be connected, because everyone on the train is from high society," Hal said. "Searching for the thief, I discovered that there was a stowaway hiding in the empty royal carriage. That's when I met Lenny, the train driver's daughter."

"Just as the inspector has said," Steven Pickle declared.

"Lenny and I became friends. I told her about the jewel thief, and together we tried to solve the case, especially after the Atlas Diamond was taken. Our first suspect was Milo Essenbach."

220

Milo looked startled as heads turned to look at him.

"We couldn't work out why he was on the train. He isn't a steam enthusiast, and he didn't seem happy. He was in the observation car when the brooch was stolen, and then I saw him hide something sparkling in his pocket that time Steven Pickle wanted to search my room. He even told the police he had no alibi for when the Atlas Diamond was taken." Hal looked at Milo. "I'm ashamed to say, we thought the scar over your lip made you look like a villain. I'm sorry—that was wrong."

"So, *he's* the thief?" Steven Pickle turned to Milo.

"No, he's not." Hal shook his head. "He gave no alibi to Inspector Clyde because he was protecting someone."

Milo stiffened. "I was?"

"I'm sorry, Milo"—Hal looked at the floor—"but I found your letter in the book in the library."

"Letter? What letter?" Baron Essenbach asked.

"Ah. Well, I suppose it had to come out sooner or later." Milo sighed. "I was going to tell you, Dad, once we'd got off this blasted train."

"Tell me what?"

"Your son came on this journey because you asked him to," Hal said to the baron, "but also to be near to the woman he loves."

"Oh no," Sierra whispered.

"Milo lied to Inspector Clyde because he was with someone while the train traveled from Ballater to Aberdeen."

"How is a detective supposed to do her job if people lie!" Inspector Clyde exclaimed.

"I thought Milo was in love with Sierra," explained Hal. "I'd seen her teasing Milo about getting married and hanging off his

221

arm . . . But he's not in love with *Sierra*," Hal said. "It's Lucy you're in love with, isn't it, Milo?"

"Oh!" Lucy's hands covered her blushing face.

"I thought Sierra had sent Lucy to collect your love letters, but the letters were for her. She went to see *you* when the train went to Aberdeen, not Sierra. Sierra's the one who didn't have an alibi, and that's why she made Lucy lie for her."

"You lied as well?" Inspector Clyde demanded, looking at Sierra.

"Sierra *wanted* an alibi," Hal continued, "because she already has a police record for shoplifting."

Lydia Pickle gasped. "I knew it! Didn't I say?" She turned to Sierra. "The gossip mags are gonna go *bonkers* if you stole the biggest diamond in the world from your best friend."

"She's the thief?" Mr. Pickle squealed, looking like he was about to have a heart attack.

"No, I'm not!" Sierra scowled.

"Milo lied to protect Lucy," Hal went on. "Sierra lied to protect herself, and she asked Lucy to lie, too." He looked at Milo. "The thing I saw you stuffing in your pocket—it was the bracelet found in the tender, and it's Lucy's." He pulled out his book and turned to his sketch of the observation car. "I even drew it on her wrist, the day we stepped onto the train—but I didn't make the connection. You were trying to return it when you met the crowd of us in the corridor. You couldn't, so you left it in your compartment—in the soap dish. The thief had plenty of time while the train sat at Ballater to see it through the window and plan to steal it later."

"How can you know about the bracelet?" Milo asked, amazed.

Hal blushed. "Lenny and I were so certain you were the thief that, when the train pulled into Settle, she climbed into your room through the window. We thought the bracelet was a clue. She had to hide in the drawer under the sofa because the *real* thief broke in and took it. When Lenny tried to leave, Sergeant Prattle saw her, found the lock forced on your door, and arrested her. The real thief threw the bracelet in the tender to give the inspector the evidence she needed to charge Mr. Singh and Lenny." Hal sighed.

"No one claimed the bracelet," he continued, "because then they'd have to explain why Lucy's bracelet was in Milo's room. It would have exposed their secret." He turned to Sierra. "But you recognized it, didn't you? You worked out what was going on." He looked at Lucy. "And that's why I heard you crying in the bathroom."

Milo reached across the table and took Lucy's hand. "You were crying?"

"I fired her," said Sierra. "She's a lying little jezebel."

"The only lie I told was the one you asked me to," said Lucy sharply.

"You stole him from me!" snapped Sierra.

"People aren't possessions, Sierra," said Milo. "I was never *yours*."

"Oh, please." Sierra shook her head. "I don't understand what you see in her. She's not even pretty."

"I think she's beautiful." Milo smiled. "And I plan on marrying her, if she'll have me."

"Oh!" Lucy blushed. "Yes, I will."

Baron Essenbach stood up. "May I be the first to congratulate you, Milo, on an excellent match." He looked at Lucy. "Welcome to the family, my dear."

Sierra looked away in disgust.

"Ahem." Lady Lansbury coughed politely. "This is all terribly interesting, but does that mean the actress took my earrings?" She turned to Sierra. "I really would rather like them back."

"I crossed Milo and Lucy off my suspect list because they had an alibi." Hal stepped forward. "Lydia Pickle and Lady Lansbury, I placed you above suspicion because you were the thief's victims and are also wealthy—I couldn't see a motive for either of you to be the thief."

"We would hardly steal our own jewels," huffed Steven Pickle.

"Or, at least, that's what I thought—until I learned you were in financial trouble, Mr. Pickle."

"I beg your pardon?"

"When the Highland Falcon left King's Cross, Ernest White installed that microphone." Hal pointed at the fluffy mic head clamped to the window. "He wanted to preserve the sound of the train's last journey, but it also recorded fragments of conversation from that table."

"He *what*?" Mr. Pickle glared at the device.

"It wasn't intended to," said Ernest unapologetically, "but you are very loud."

"Grailax badly needs money," Hal said, "and Mr. Pickle came on this trip hoping to persuade Baron Essenbach and Lady Lansbury to invest in his company."

"Did you, babes?" Lydia Pickle asked, blinking. "I thought it was 'cause you wanted to see the castle."

"Those were private conversations!" Mr. Pickle blustered.

"It was possible you'd steal your wife's brooch to collect the insurance," said Hal. "It would also divert attention from you when the Atlas Diamond was stolen, too."

Lydia Pickle gasped. "You *never*!"

"You brat!" Steven Pickle slammed his hand on the table. "This is outrageous. I'll sue you for slander, you little maggot!"

"You became my number one suspect." Hal didn't break eye contact with Steven Pickle, enjoying the moment. "You were in the observation car when the brooch was stolen. You have no real alibi for the time the princess's necklace was taken. You had a motive, and you were constantly trying to cast suspicion on me." Steven Pickle's face was turning purple. "But despite all that," Hal concluded, "it didn't fit. Whoever swapped the necklace for a fake did it swiftly and silently. The crime was meticulously planned by someone very clever. It couldn't have been you."

Steven Pickle's mouth opened and closed like a goldfish, and Amy let out a snort of laughter.

"I suspected all of you, even my own uncle," Hal said to the room. "There was only one person I knew for certain didn't commit the crime, and that was Marlene Singh." He turned to Inspector Clyde. "Because we were eating scones in the generator room while we traveled back from Ballater."

Inspector Clyde put her head in her hands. "Did any of you tell me the truth?"

"I went round and round trying to work out who could have hidden in the princess's wardrobe and switched the pendants. Who had a key? Who had the opportunity? The fake copy of the necklace had to have been made in advance by someone very skilled. The crime had been carefully planned. But what a silly plan—to hide in a wardrobe waiting for the princess and her guard to leave the necklace alone at the right moment. Who would plan a crime like that? And then I realized—nobody would. Because that's not when the necklace was taken."

Inspector Clyde looked up. "What?"

"Stealing a brooch from someone—while they're still wearing it," Hal said. "That's the sign of a skilled pickpocket. Someone who sees something they want and takes it, using nimble fingers and misdirection." He shook his head. "That's when I realized the diamond necklace must have been stolen before the princess even got on the train. It was stolen at Balmoral."

"That's impossible." Heads turned at the sound of the prince's voice.

"Your Royal Highness." Hal bowed his head.

"My wife took the necklace from the safe before any of you arrived at Balmoral," the prince said. "It was around her neck in plain sight of many people, including myself, the whole time. She didn't take it off until we were in the train carriage."

"Exactly," said Hal. "That's why no one thought it could have been taken sooner . . . but it was."

"When was it stolen, Harrison?" The princess came to stand beside her husband.

"It was stolen from your neck in front of everybody," said Hal, "by a skillful criminal. Someone who's been stealing the jewels of her friends in high society for years." He turned and pointed. "It was stolen by Lady Lansbury."

CHAPTER THIRTY-TWO

OFF THE RAILS

ady Lansbury laughed. "You can't be serious, boy!"

"You were a guest at every one of the parties where the jewel thief struck," Hal said.

"I'm invited to every society occasion," Lady Lansbury said, "but that doesn't make me a thief. I was a victim of the thief, remember?"

"I do remember." Hal nodded, lifting his drawing. "I remember you wore black dangling earrings in the observation car. The ones you're wearing now look like emeralds surrounded by diamonds." He flipped the pages to a profile sketch of her. "And you wore huge square earrings to Balmoral."

"Well, I have many pairs of earrings in my jewelry box."

"Exactly. Then why didn't the thief take them all?" Hal asked.

There was a stunned silence.

"Why would a thief steal only one pair of pearl earrings, when there were giant diamonds on offer? I think your earrings were never taken. You invented a theft to put yourself above suspicion."

"This is preposterous." Lady Lansbury looked at the princess.

"Are you suggesting that I ripped the pendant from the princess's neck? I'm certain she would have noticed."

"You didn't rip it from her neck," Hal said, "and you didn't act alone."

"I'm tired. I'm returning to my compartment."

"You had help from your son, Terrence Lansbury. Or, as we've known him on the Highland Falcon, Rowan Buck, your gentleman-in-waiting."

"Terry?" The prince turned and stared. "My God—is it you?"

"He kept away from everyone as much as possible, but especially you," Hal said, as Lady Lansbury's son's head dropped. "He's lost weight and dyed his hair, but there was a risk you'd recognize him. Isaac gave me this old photograph of the prince with his family standing by the Highland Falcon." Hal held it up. "Lady Lansbury: this is you, your husband, your daughter, and your son." He looked at the man he'd known as Rowan Buck. "You were chubby and smiley, without the mustache, but it's the same face—just older. I realized when I drew you."

"*So what?*" spluttered Lady Lansbury. "My son is here, looking after my dogs. The poor boy just got out of prison. He needed a job—I thought it would be terribly embarrassing for him to be here as a servant under his own name, so we pretended he was someone else. That's not a crime. It's charitable."

"But why do you have *dogs*, Lady Lansbury?" asked Hal. "You don't seem to like them. You get their names wrong, and your son doesn't treat them well. Dogs don't like being shut up on a train for days, so why would you bring them?" Hal felt himself getting angry. "You have the dogs because you needed them to make the crime work." He shook his head.

"When they got on the train, I thought the dogs were naughty, but if I asked them to sit, they did it. I thought it was because they liked me, but they responded to Rowan's whistle when he took them to the bathroom, so why did he struggle to keep them under control the rest of the time? Unless he was pretending."

"But those mutts attack me every time they see me!" exclaimed Sierra.

"On my first night on the train, I visited the compartment where the dogs are kept and drew them." Hal flipped the pages of his sketchbook. "I saw bottles of Gyastara perfume by the sink."

"That's my perfume," said the princess.

"Mine, too," said Sierra.

"Rowan—I mean, Terrence— trained the Samoyeds to jump and bark and fuss whenever they smelled the princess's perfume. He didn't realize Sierra wore it as well, but it didn't matter. What mattered was that the dogs would crowd around the princess." He looked at her. "At Balmoral, you said you loved Samoyeds—is that right?"

The princess nodded. "I had one when I was a girl."

"Lady Lansbury knew that. She counted on you hugging them when they ran to you—that you wouldn't run away."

"Why would my liking Samoyeds help them steal my necklace?" asked the princess.

"Watch," said Hal. "Uncle Nat?"

Uncle Nat reached into his jacket and pulled out a bottle of Gyastara perfume, which he tossed across the carriage to Hal with a wink. Hal spritzed the perfume into the air, and immediately four of the dogs yapped and jumped against their leashes, held back by Terrence Lansbury. Only Bailey didn't leap about, but lay at his feet, whimpering.

"When the dogs were taken out of the car at Balmoral, they smelled your perfume and rushed toward you," Hal explained to the princess. "Terrence pretended he couldn't control them, but they were trained to knock you over. Lady Lansbury rushed over and put her arm around you. She was behind you, Rowan was in front, and for a moment, none of us could see you.

"Everyone was surprised and concerned, and in the commotion, with quick, light fingers, Lady Lansbury took the fake necklace from her purse, undid the clasp, and switched them—putting the Atlas pendant in her clutch bag. When they helped you to your feet, you were wearing the copy. Lady Lansbury gave Terrence her purse with the real necklace inside and sent him back to the train. It happened in full view—and none of us noticed."

Lady Lansbury started clapping very slowly and rose out of her seat, stepping toward him. "A marvelous story," she said, looking unconcerned, "but utter nonsense. Why would I steal jewelry when I own more jewels than the queen herself? I have no need of them. My late husband, the Count of Arundel, was one of the wealthiest men in the country."

"He might have been once," said Hal, "but he left you with a mansion to run—and enormous debts. Isaac said something that stuck in my head: *Whoever forged the necklace was an artist.* This isn't the first time you've arranged to have glass copies made, is it?

How much of your own jewelry have you had to sell and replace with fakes? I suppose that's where you got the idea."

"Poppycock!" Lady Lansbury declared.

"And yet very plausible," said Inspector Clyde, getting to her feet.

"Then where is the necklace?" Lady Lansbury asked triumphantly. "Where is the brooch? Where are all these jewels I've apparently stolen?"

"Here," said Lenny, coming out from her hiding place and holding up the blue suitcase.

"You're supposed to be in the luggage cage," said Inspector Clyde.

"What is that smell?" asked Baron Essenbach, wrinkling his nose.

"The cleverest and cruelest bit of your plan is how you fooled a team of sniffer dogs. You didn't just use your dogs to steal the jewels," Hal said, feeling the anger rising in his gut, "you used them to hide them. After you'd taken Lydia Pickle's brooch, Terrence wrapped it up in a piece of roast beef and fed it to Viking. You did the same with the necklace—you broke the chain into pieces and fed it to the dogs. That's why Terrence has been following the dogs around on their toilet breaks, collecting, bagging, and tagging all of their poo."

Lenny snapped open the blue suitcase to reveal the squidgy black bags with white labels. A shudder of disgust rippled through the guests.

"Each label says which dog the poo is from. You planned to go through the bags when you got home and dig out everything you stole."

231

"Eurgh—that is rank!" Lydia Pickle made a face. "I feel sick."

"But the Atlas Diamond is big," Hal said. "You fed it to Bailey, and it's made her ill. Look at her. The diamond is hurting her."

"Oh no!" The princess rushed to Bailey and dropped to her knees. The dog looked up at her with a forlorn face.

"Inspector Clyde, if you look through the bags in this suitcase, I'm sure you'll find the brooch and pieces of the necklace." Hal took the open suitcase from Lenny and passed it to the detective. "You may even find the Duchess of Kent's ruby ring."

"This sounds like a job for Sergeant Prattle," said Inspector Clyde, promptly handing the poo over to her unimpressed detective sergeant.

"I'm not sure I want that brooch back now," said Lydia Pickle, wrinkling her nose.

"We're getting it back," said Mr. Pickle.

"Lady Lansbury and Terrence Lansbury, you are both under arrest," said Inspector Clyde, stepping forward. "When we reach Paddington, you'll be taken in for questioning. Until then, you will both be confined to your compartments."

"I don't think so."

Lady Lansbury grabbed the bottle of Gyastara perfume from Hal and sprayed it into Inspector Clyde's eyes, then hurled it at the floor, where it smashed. The dogs exploded with energy, barking and jumping onto the inspector, who crashed into a table, blinded. In the commotion, Lady Lansbury reached up and pulled the emergency brake cord.

The vacuum brakes in the Highland Falcon slammed shut, and the wheels locked. There was a horrific squealing noise, and a wall of force shoved glasses and crockery off tables, smashing onto the floor. The guests gripped the arms of their chairs. Sergeant Prattle lost his balance, and the suitcase flew forward, bags of poo spinning out in all directions. Steven Pickle roared as a bag hit his forehead, burst, and splattered everywhere.

Lady Lansbury leaped across the carriage, shoving the princess aside and scooping up Bailey from the floor.

"Stop her!" Uncle Nat called out, stumbling after her, as Lady Lansbury and the dog vanished into the King Edward Saloon.

Hal pulled Lenny to her feet, and the three of them struggled forward, bracing themselves against the walls as the carriages juddered and screeched. Through the library and the game room, they pursued the countess, rushing into the observation car as the train finally stopped.

Lady Lansbury was opening the doors to the veranda.

"Please, Countess!" Uncle Nat shouted. "Give yourself up. You've nowhere to go."

"I'm not going to prison," she snapped back, hiking up her skirt and jumping down onto the railway line. She dropped Bailey to the ground and yanked her by the leash.

Rushing to the veranda, Hal, Lenny, and Uncle Nat saw Lady Lansbury picking her way along a parallel track, one arm held out for balance, the other dragging Bailey behind her.

"We're between Chippenham and Swindon," said Uncle Nat, looking at the yellow fields of wheat stretching away from them in every direction. "No, Hal." Uncle Nat grabbed Hal's arm to stop him from pursuing Lady Lansbury onto the tracks. "We're on the main line. It's dangerous—trains come along here at more than a hundred miles an hour. Wait for the police—she can't get far."

"Up here!" Lenny was clambering up the white ladder and onto the roof. "We can see where she goes."

Hal looked at his uncle.

Uncle Nat nodded. "I'll wait here for the police."

Hal scrambled up the ladder and followed Lenny as she walked along the central ironwork strip of the observation-car roof. With the train stopped, there was no sound but the whispering of the wheat.

"There she is." Lenny pointed and jumped over to the roof of the saloon.

"What's she doing?" Hal stared at Lady Lansbury, who was two tracks over and had stopped moving.

"Has she got her foot stuck?" asked Lenny.

"No—it's Bailey," said Hal. "Look."

Lady Lansbury was tugging furiously at Bailey's leash. But the dog wouldn't budge.

They heard the blast of a train horn in the distance.

"That's an InterCity 125!" Lenny cried. "It'll be here any minute!"

But Hal was already shinning down the ladder between the observation car and the saloon. He dropped to the ground and sprinted out over the ballast.

"Hal, no!" Lenny shouted.

He kept running—there was no time to look back. He could see Lady Lansbury struggling with the leash.

"Get off the track!" he shouted. The rails beneath them were vibrating. "There's a train coming!"

"Come on, you dumb hound!" shouted Lady Lansbury, tugging on Bailey's leash. "I command you."

Bailey looked terrified, lying huddled on her front, braced against the rail, refusing to move as the diesel express raced toward them at high speed. Its horn blared, and Lady Lansbury's head snapped up, staring the train in the face—but still she didn't drop the leash.

"LET GO!" Hal screamed, leaping forward and grabbing Bailey by the collar, hugging the dog to his body as he hurled himself across the rails and into Lady Lansbury, knocking her backward off her feet. They all toppled over, rolling away from the track as the express rocketed past. A deafening shock wave flattened the long grass beside them.

"Hal?" He heard his uncle's voice. "Oh dear God, no! *Hal!*"

"Over here," Lady Lansbury said with a voice like vinegar. "He's alive. As am I."

Bailey licked Hal's face, and he drew her in for a hug.

A line of police sprang from the train. Sergeant Prattle was pushing Terrence Lansbury, who was wearing handcuffs.

"You stupid boy!" Uncle Nat ran across the tracks. "What did you do that for?" There were tears streaking down his cheeks. "I thought I'd lost you." He knelt down and hugged Hal.

"She was going to get killed," Hal said weakly. "I thought the police would come."

"They were waiting for the train to pass."

"Mother!" Terrence Lansbury fell to his knees beside Lady Lansbury.

She put her hand to his cheek. Two police officers helped the countess to her feet and cuffed her. Terrence looked over at Hal.

"Thank you. You saved my mother's life. I know you think we're nothing but thieves, but she's my mom, and she's always tried to do her best for us."

As the other guests stared out through the windows of the dining car, Hal found himself being wrapped in a blanket. Inspector Clyde gathered Bailey carefully in her arms, and Uncle Nat insisted on carrying Hal back to their compartment, where a police officer talked to him about shock.

The Highland Falcon began to move again, chuffing toward Paddington on the last stretch of her final journey.

CHAPTER THIRTY-THREE

NEXT STOP

Enormous crowds were gathered under the high arches of Paddington station to welcome the Highland Falcon. Hal stepped out of the dining car onto the red carpet, his yellow jacket on, his rucksack on his back. Only four days had passed since he'd climbed aboard, but the Highland Falcon felt like an old friend, and he was sad to say goodbye. Uncle Nat stood beside him, umbrella over his arm and suitcase in his hand.

Lenny leaped down from the footplate, running along the platform toward him. "Dad wants to speak to you!" she shouted.

Mohanjit Singh appeared through a cloud of steam, no longer in handcuffs. The train driver walked toward them. "Harrison Beck." He shook Hal's hand. "I'll never be able to thank you enough for what you've done for me and my daughter. You'll always be welcome in my house, and on the footplate of any locomotive I drive." He looked Hal in the eye. "But if I ever, *ever* hear of you climbing on top of a train running at fifty miles an hour, I will—"

"I beg your pardon?" Uncle Nat looked startled.

"Ha, ha—he's joking." Hal looked at Lenny's dad with pleading eyes. "Aren't you, Mr. Singh?"

Lenny's dad patted Hal's shoulder. "A little joke, Mr. Bradshaw."

"Good." Uncle Nat put his hand over his heart. "Bev would never speak to me again."

"We want you to come and stay when Dad starts his new job," Lenny said, bouncing up and down. "He's going to teach us how to drive the engine."

There was a roar from the crowd as the prince stepped off the train. He held out his hand for the princess, and she appeared, waving to the cheering crowd.

"Harrison Beck and Marlene Singh," the prince called, beckoning them over.

Uncle Nat gave them a little shove.

Lenny grabbed Hal's hand as they approached the prince and princess.

"Thanks to your friendship, bravery, and powers of deduction, the Atlas Diamond will soon be safely back with the crown jewels." The prince smiled. "The Duchess of Kent will be rewarding you for catching the notorious jewel thief who stole her ruby ring . . ."

"We get the reward?" Lenny squealed.

The prince nodded. "But I want to thank you personally." He put his hand in his jacket pocket and pulled out a shining silver whistle. "This railway whistle once belonged to my father." The prince flipped over the whistle, and Hal saw it was engraved with the words *The Highland Falcon*. The prince held it out. "I want you to have it."

"Thank you, sir . . . Your Highness, Royalness, Prince, sir," Lenny babbled, as she reached out and took the whistle.

"Take good care of it," the prince said.

"Is this the same whistle that . . . I mean . . . Ernest White told us a story about how your dad accidentally . . . ," Hal spluttered.

The prince nodded. "My great-grandmother never forgave him."

"Aren't you sad that the Highland Falcon's going to a museum?" Hal asked, looking past the prince at the claret locomotive.

"Everyone can enjoy her in the museum, Harrison." The prince smiled again. "You can visit her anytime you like."

The princess bent down, kissing Lenny and then Hal on the cheeks. There were flashes as people took pictures. "If there's anything we can do for you," she said, "you must ask."

"I do want to know one thing," Hal said. "What will happen to Lady Lansbury's dogs?"

"You mustn't worry." The princess smiled. "I'm going to take care of them."

"But I was wondering . . . If my parents let me, do you think I'd be allowed to give Bailey a home?"

"I'm sure Bailey would love that." The princess nodded. "First the royal vet will examine the dogs," she continued. "We're a little worried about what they have in their tummies. But once they've been given a clean bill of health, we'll be in touch with you."

"Thank you." Hal beamed and then bowed, unsure of the proper way to thank a royal person.

"Goodbye," the prince and princess said in unison. Then they smiled, joined hands, and walked toward the cheering crowds and television cameras.

Lenny stared down at the whistle in her hand. "We'll share it. You have it for six months, and then I'll have it for six months. That way we have to see each other. Deal?"

"Deal," said Hal. "But you take it first, because I'm getting Bailey." His eyes flickered across the crowd. "If Dad says yes."

"C'mon, Hal," Uncle Nat called. "Your mom'll be looking for you."

"Bye, then," Lenny said.

Hal nodded. "See you."

He turned and spotted his mother's face shining like a beacon in the crowd, and he ran toward her.

"Hal!" His mom grabbed him over the rope cordon, pulling him into a warm hug. "Oh, I've missed you, petal. Have you grown again?" she chided. "You've been gone only four days."

"Sorry." Hal smiled, enjoying his mom's fussing.

"I've got someone for you to meet," she said, turning around. "Colin?"

Hal's dad stepped forward, holding a tiny baby wrapped in a white blanket.

"This is Ellie," his dad said, passing her to Hal, "your little sister. Fold your arms a bit—make sure to support her head. That's it."

Ellie was warm and smelled like milk and talcum powder. Her eyes were closed, and her mouth was moving in a slow whimper.

240

As Hal looked down at his little sister, all the noise of the busy station faded away.

"Hi, Ellie," he whispered. "I'm your big brother. I'm going to take care of you and teach you all about steam trains."

"Journey all right, Nathaniel?" his dad asked.

"It was an adventure," said Uncle Nat. "I think it will make a great book."

"I hope he wasn't any bother," his mom added.

"Quite the opposite." Uncle Nat ruffled Hal's hair. "I'd be happy to take him anytime."

"Really?" Hal's head shot up. "When?"

"I'm planning a trip on the California Comet across America." There was a twinkle in Uncle Nat's eyes. "Fancy it?"

Hal grinned. "You bet."

AUTHORS' NOTE

Dear Reader,

We have tried to be faithful and accurate in our depiction of the United Kingdom's railways in *The Highland Falcon Thief*. However, we must admit to having taken one or two liberties for the sake of a good story. We hope you will forgive us our deviations from the truth, which we confess in full here:

Aberdeen to Ballater

Sadly, you can no longer take a train from Aberdeen to Ballater to visit the Queen at Balmoral—though you can walk most of the way on a path called the Deeside Way where the track used to be. The Deeside Line was closed to passengers in 1966. A small portion of it runs today as a heritage line called the Royal Deeside Railway. Ballater station is still there but is now a museum.

With the exception of the Deeside Line, it is possible to travel most of the Highland Falcon's journey yourself. Sam worked out the route—including the sticky bit at Inverness—by modelling it with Brio with the help of his mom and dad on their living room carpet. There are places the train would need to turn around that we haven't described in detail because we didn't want to slow down the story.

The Water Trough

There are no longer water troughs on the East Coast Main Line. The line is now electrified. The troughs disappeared long ago, but we thought they were an amazing part of traveling by steam train. We put one in this story so that Hal could witness something marvelous on the footplate.

The Highland Falcon

The Highland Falcon only exists in this story. We chose an A4 Pacific as the locomotive to pull the royal train because it has a distinctive streamlined shape and was designed (by Sir Nigel Gresley) for speed. The most famous A4 Pacific is the Mallard, which holds the world record for the fastest steam engine.

Many A4 Pacific locomotives were named after birds. We decided to name the Highland Falcon after the peregrine falcon, which can be found in the Scottish Highlands, because they are one of the fastest animals on the planet, able to dive at speeds of two hundred miles per hour—quicker than the fastest steam train.

Our locomotive may be fictional, but there has been a royal train of carriages since 1842, during the reign of Queen Victoria, and in 1961 an A4 Pacific pulled the royal train when the royal family attended the wedding of the Duke of Kent at York Minster.

Find out more . . .

If you would like to learn more about trains, we recommend a trip to the York Railway Museum. You can step onto the footplate of Mallard, a real A4 Pacific, and see royal carriages. It's where Maya fell in love with trains.

ACKNOWLEDGMENTS

M. G. Leonard

When my friend, Sam Sedgman, asked me what I was going to write next, I told him I wanted to write an adventure series set on trains. The reason for this was that my children loved Thomas the Tank Engine, Duplo, Hornby, and Lego locomotives, but when my eldest was old enough to choose his own books and he searched for chapter books about trains, he found none that gave him the realism, the route, the facts, and the locomotive details he wanted, using the vocabulary he possessed and enjoyed. I wanted to write *that* book, but I couldn't, because I knew nothing about railways. Sam erupted with enthusiasm for the idea, saying he would have loved such a book when he was a boy and that I should write it immediately. He suggested types of mysteries, the amazing trains they could take place on, and the routes they might travel, and it was immediately clear to me that Adventures on Trains would only be possible if Sam agreed to write the stories with me. And so, I asked him, and our journey together began.

Creating these stories has been a delight. Sam is a wonderful writing partner, a fantastic friend, a delightful co-conspirator, hardworking, optimistic, and generous. I am grateful for everything these books have brought into my life, but in particular the opportunity to work with Sam, who has ignited a lifelong passion for railways in me.

A hearty thank-you goes to my beta readers: my husband, Sam Sparling, and my best friend, Claire Rakich, who have both loved this book since the first draft and cheered me on through my many insecure moments.

I am eternally grateful to my husband, who works with me, supports me, and believes in me more than anyone ever has. This book is, in no small part, for the boy he is at heart, a boy who loves trains.

I wish to thank my father-in-law, John Sparling, for enthusiastically sharing his knowledge (and his friends' knowledge), posting me train-related cuttings, and correcting my errors.

I would also like to say a big thank-you to Tom Leaper and Francis and Cynthia Sedgman for putting up with me in their spare room, enabling our writing sessions, and feeding me delicious food.

Huge thanks to our kick-ass agent, Kirsty McLachlan, for seeing the potential in this idea, encouraging my and Sam's collaboration, and finding Adventures on Trains a wonderful home at Macmillan.

Continuing thanks and gratitude to Lucy Pearse (our brilliant train-loving editor), Kat, Jo, Venetia, and all the great people working at Macmillan, thank you for all your hard work and your love for trains. We salute you.

Sam Sedgman

I must start with my brilliant parents, without whom this book would not exist. I have them to thank for always doing everything they could to fill my imagination to the brim with books, adventures, the time and space to play. They took me on holiday to places with steam railways and to see murder mysteries at the theatre. They took me to hedge mazes, played the games I made up, and helped me name characters in my notebook at the seaside. This book is the book I always wanted to read and you have given me everything I needed to write it. Thank you, thank you, thank you.

I would be lost without my wonderful partner, Tom Leaper. Tom gets it. Tom understands that living with a temperamental creative person is a nightmare, but loves me anyway. Thank you for being my cheerleader, for making me laugh, and for making me believe I could do it. I love you.

I have always written, but I have not always been good at it. Thank you to everyone who has helped me get better—especially Mrs. Lunnon, who mortified me by reading my story out in front of the entire class, and persuaded me to study English.

Thank you to Emma Reidy, the third member of our dream team, for tireless enthusiasm. Thank you to Sam Sparling for all the delicious meals. And thank you to Uncle David for building an enormous model railway in your barn and showing me trains were something fun that grown-ups could take seriously.

Publishing is a bewildering world and I am immensely grateful to have the support of my agent, Kirsty McLachlan, who has worked tirelessly and unflappably to support this project and find it a welcoming home at Macmillan. Macmillan themselves deserve perpetual thanks—thank you to the supreme Lucy Pearse for being the kindest editor we could hope for, and to Venetia, Jo, Kat, and the rest of the team who continue to do so much for us.

But mostly, I must thank Maya. After appearing like a fairy godmother in my hour of need and offering me my first real job, she quickly went from being the best boss I'd ever had to one of my greatest friends. Working with her has been the highlight of this whole process. Her fierce work ethic, generosity, and insight leave me in constant awe, and it has been a privilege to be her partner in crime. Maya, thank you for changing my life several times.

THANK YOU FOR READING THIS FEIWEL AND FRIENDS BOOK.

The Friends who made

possible are:

JEAN FEIWEL, Publisher

LIZ SZABLA, Associate Publisher

RICH DEAS, Senior Creative Director

HOLLY WEST, Senior Editor

ANNA ROBERTO, Senior Editor

KAT BRZOZOWSKI, Senior Editor

DAWN RYAN, Senior Managing Editor

KIM WAYMER, Senior Production Manager

EMILY SETTLE, Associate Editor

ERIN SIU, Associate Editor

RACHEL DIEBEL, Assistant Editor

FOYINSI ADEGBONMIRE, Editorial Assistant

KATIE KLIMOWICZ, Senior Designer

LINDSAY WAGNER, Production Editor

FOLLOW US ON FACEBOOK OR VISIT US ONLINE AT MACKIDS.COM

OUR BOOKS ARE FRIENDS FOR LIFE.